Mother smiles. "You have a gift, hijica. Keep on writing your poems."

We both settle back into our writing, the light of the afternoon illuminating our words. As I write, I think about how they can take away my home but not my words, the words that form themselves into poems.

I promise myself I will hold on to my language, no matter how far away we go, how many seas we cross, how distant I am from the almond-scented streets of this land. Even at the ends of the earth, I will remember where I came from.

ALSO BY RUTH BEHAR

Letters from Cuba
Lucky Broken Girl
Tía Fortuna's New Home

ACROSS SO MANY SEAS

RUTH BEHAR

Nancy Paulsen Books

NANCY PAULSEN BOOKS
An imprint of Penguin Random House LLC
1745 Broadway, New York, New York 10019

First published in the United States of America by Nancy Paulsen Books,
an imprint of Penguin Random House LLC, 2024
First paperback edition published 2025

Copyright © 2024 by Ruth Behar

Penguin Random House values and supports copyright. Copyright fuels creativity, encourages diverse voices, promotes free speech, and creates a vibrant culture. Thank you for buying an authorized edition of this book and for complying with copyright laws by not reproducing, scanning, or distributing any part of it in any form without permission. You are supporting writers and allowing Penguin Random House to continue to publish books for every reader. Please note that no part of this book may be used or reproduced in any manner for the purpose of training artificial intelligence technologies or systems.

Nancy Paulsen Books & colophon are trademarks of Penguin Random House LLC.
The Penguin colophon is a registered trademark of Penguin Books Limited.

Visit us online at PenguinRandomHouse.com.

The Library of Congress has cataloged the hardcover edition as follows:
Names: Behar, Ruth.
Title: Across so many seas / Ruth Behar.
Description: New York: Nancy Paulsen Books, 2024. | Includes bibliographical references. | Summary: "Spanning over five hundred years, a novel telling the stories of four girls from different generations of a Jewish family, many of them forced to leave their country and start a new life"—Provided by publisher.
Identifiers: LCCN 2023010433 | ISBN 9780593323403 (hardcover) | ISBN 9780593323410 (ebook)
Subjects: CYAC: Jews—Fiction. | Family life—Fiction. | Refugees—Fiction. | LCGFT: Novels.
Classification: LCC PZ7.1.B447 Ac 2024 | DDC [Fic]—dc23
LC record available at https://lccn.loc.gov/2023010433

Manufactured in the United States of America

ISBN 9780593323427
1st Printing

LSCC

Edited by Nancy Paulsen
Design by Marikka Tamura
Text set in Tisa Pro

This is a work of historical fiction. Apart from the well-known actual people, events, and locales that figure in the narrative, all names, characters, places, and incidents are the products of the author's imagination or are used fictitiously. Any resemblance to current events or locales, or to living persons, is entirely coincidental.

The publisher does not have any control over and does not assume any responsibility for author or third-party websites or their content.

The authorized representative in the EU for product safety and compliance is Penguin Random House Ireland, Morrison Chambers, 32 Nassau Street, Dublin D02 YH68, Ireland, https://eu-contact.penguin.ie.

*In memory of Abuela and her oud,
and to my granddaughters, Mila and Colette,
with love and hope*

CONTENTS

PART ONE: BENVENIDA, 1492

1. The Proclamation . . . 1
2. Expulsion . . . 3
3. They Can Take Away My Home but Not My Words . . . 7
4. We Don't Moan About What We Have Lost . . . 12
5. A Taste of Sweetness as Life Grows Bitter . . . 15
6. Singing, We Leave Toledo . . . 19
7. Sleep, Sleep, Without Fear and Pain . . . 23
8. She Will Be Called Preciada . . . 27
9. The Forest . . . 32
10. Adiós, Amina, Adiós . . . 36
11. Open a Road Through the Sea . . . 40
12. Pray Our Broken Souls Will Heal . . . 43
13. Remember, Hijica, Live the Truth of Who You Are . . . 47
14. I Carry My Tambourine . . . 51
15. Poems That She Wore Like Jewels . . . 57
16. A Reunion Amid Eggplants . . . 62
17. I Will Lift My Voice and Be Heard . . . 65

PART TWO: REINA, 1923

18. I Came Into the World Carrying a Bundle of Sadness . . . 71
19. The Parade . . . 75
20. I Believe I Should Be Free . . . 79
21. In the Sea There Is a Tower . . . 83

22. I'll Keep Listening to You Through the Walls . . . 88
23. To Me, You Are Dead . . . 92
24. Once You Are There, Don't Look Back, Hijica . . . 94
25. Song of the Sisters . . . 98
26. Sadik's Goodbye . . . 101
27. Take the Key . . . 103
28. Throw Your Oud Into the Sea . . . 106
29. The Breezes Are Soothing, Morning and Night . . . 109
30. She Is a Melancholy One, Isn't She? . . . 112

PART THREE: ALEGRA, 1961
31. I Have Tasted Mamá's Tears in the Food I Eat . . . 119
32. I Imagine Her Heart Traveling . . . 123
33. Love on Shabbat . . . 127
34. Baklava and Batá Drums on Calle Oficios . . . 130
35. One Less Secret . . . 134
36. Enjoy Your Freedom . . . 138
37. As Cuban as the Palm Trees . . . 142
38. Holding Up Our Books . . . 147
39. A Man Who Can Make Us Shout Until We Have No Voice . . . 151
40. Born on an Island . . . 156
41. Teach Us . . . 159
42. In a House With Total Strangers . . . 162
43. The Well . . . 167
44. And What Is That Star You Wear Around Your Neck? . . . 171
45. Zunzuncito . . . 175
46. An Alarming Letter . . . 178
47. A Handful of Mangos . . . 180

48. It Is Time for You to Sing Again . . . 183
49. We Will Be Together Soon . . . 188
50. Please Don't Make Me an Orphan . . . 191

PART FOUR: PALOMA, 2003
51. So Much Had to Happen Before I Could Be Born . . . 197
52. Keeper of Memories . . . 202
53. You Must Learn the Song and Remember It by Heart . . . 206
54. A Tale Across Five Hundred Years . . . 211
55. Maybe Lorca's Ghost Has Met the Ghosts of My Ancestors . . . 213
56. We'll Be Surrounded by History There . . . 216
57. Are You Ready for the Tour? . . . 218
58. If You Ever Hear from Reina Cohen Toledano . . . 224
59. A Lost Country . . . 228
60. The Scent of Almonds and Honey . . . 231
61. Toledo Won't Ever Forget You . . . 235

AUTHOR'S NOTE . . . 237
SOURCES . . . 245
ACKNOWLEDGMENTS . . . 253

In the first week of July they took the route for quitting their native land and set off upon the hardships of the road, the small and great, old and young, on foot and riding donkeys and other beasts of burden, and on carts, to the ports from which they were to leave. They traveled along the roads and through the fields with great difficulty and misfortune, some falling and others rising, some dying, others being born and others falling ill, until there was no Christian who did not grieve for them. Wherever they went, they were offered baptism, and some in their affliction converted and stayed behind, but very few. The rabbis encouraged them, and they made the women and young people sing and play tambourines and timbrels to keep up their spirits . . .

—*From a chronicle of the 1492 expulsion*

PART ONE

Benvenida
1492

1

The Proclamation

The sound of trumpets coming from the direction of our town gates tears me from sleep, my dreams forgotten as I jolt out of bed.

My whole family dresses quickly as the sun begins to rise. Then I follow Mother and Father and my brothers, Isaac and Jacob, to the Plaza Mayor.

"Hurry, Benvenida," Mother says, turning around. "Don't dawdle. We don't want to miss any announcements."

Hearing my name usually makes me smile—as the youngest and only girl of the family, I was named Benvenida because everyone welcomed me when I was born.

But today is not a day for smiles.

The cobblestoned path, glistening from the morning dew, is slippery under my feet. It is strange to be out this early, but the familiar scent of almond sweets that perfumes our town calms me.

As we join the hundreds of townspeople gathered in the Plaza Mayor, we watch the solemn procession approach.

At the front marches a line of Catholic priests carrying the green cross of the Holy Office of the Inquisition. Behind them, soldiers with swords at their sides.

The sun shines brightly, but the last gasp of winter air makes the day feel chilly. I draw closer to Mother to stay warm.

"Mother, what is happening? Why must we be here?"

She whispers, "The rumor is that King Fernando and Queen Isabel will now insist on uniting the kingdom under the Catholic faith, which means things will get even worse for us as Jews. Let's hope that rumor is false."

We wait as the officer at arms, dressed in a black robe and white collar, takes his place at the center of the Plaza Mayor and unrolls a parchment. Slowly he reads aloud a proclamation, shouting in Spanish:

"On this day, the thirty-first of March of the year 1492, we order all Jews and Jewesses, regardless of age, who live in our kingdoms and lordships . . . that by the end of the month of July of the present year, they depart from all of these our realms and lordships . . . And whoever disobeys us and does not leave within this time and is to be found in any place in our kingdom will be sentenced to death by hanging . . ."

A gasp arises from the crowd.

I can see the Jews around me lowering their eyes at the indignity.

Echoing in my heart, those words . . . *death by hanging* . . .

I shake with fear as we head home, hardly believing what I've just heard.

2

Expulsion

Father closes the door swiftly the minute we arrive home, and we all slip into the kitchen, the room farthest from the street, where we can speak without being heard by neighbors.

"You know what they're calling for?" Father asks Mother, clutching his chest.

"Expulsion," she replies solemnly.

"What does *expulsion* mean?" I ask.

Isaac, who is fifteen and knows the answers to most anything, says, "It means we Jews are to be thrown out of the kingdom. We have to leave by the end of July—that's only four months."

"How can that be? Hasn't our family lived in Toledo for hundreds of years? Don't we belong here?"

"Yes, we do belong here," says Jacob, who knows almost as much as Isaac, just having celebrated his bar mitzvah. "But they will only let us stay if we convert to Catholicism."

"And that we will never do!" I exclaim.

I've heard Father say this many times, even though in

our own family there are converts, called *conversos*. To Father's great shame, his two sisters and their families accepted baptism to the Catholic faith. "I thank the Lord that our parents are no longer alive, for they would cry without end for my sisters," Father had said when they began to wear crosses around their necks.

Life would be easier if we converted, though. Around us are family, friends, and neighbors who gave up being Jewish in the hope that they wouldn't stand out as different.

The friends I played with as a small child, two sisters called Susanah and Deborah, no longer speak to me. Yet not so long ago, the three of us were best friends. We ate together, prayed together, dreamed together. As little girls, we chased one another on the streets, skinning our knees, and kissing one another's wounds so they'd heal.

At first, after they converted, I thought I'd done something to make them angry. I tried to ask for forgiveness by giving them candied figs.

"Stay away!" they yelled. "We can't be friends with you until you stop being a Jew."

And I yelled back, "Then we shall never be friends!"

I pitied them for turning against their own religion and forsaking our traditions. I wondered what that must feel like and wrote a poem about it:

> *I fear for all*
> *who hide their faith.*

Do their tears burn
as they fall down their cheeks?

Poems come into my head all the time, and I usually try to write them down. I am fortunate Mother comes from a family of book printers and has taught me to read and write in Hebrew and Spanish. I even know a little Arabic, because Mother shared with me the verses of Qasmuna, the Jewish poet who once lived in Granada—the land that King Fernando and Queen Isabel seized a few months ago from the Moors. *I'm dark-eyed just like you, and lonely,* Qasmuna wrote—and it felt like she was talking to me. However, I must not speak about these things, because females are not supposed to read, but Father respects Mother's family background and doesn't object to her teaching me. Writing poems, though, is a high art, which he thinks is best left to men.

Now Father pulls at his robe so sharply that the fabric rips. Then he breaks into a song, borrowed from a psalm, a tune so sad tears come to all of our eyes.

Be merciful unto me, O God, be merciful unto me:
for my soul trusts in you.
In the shadow of your wings
will I make my refuge
until these calamities shall be overcome.

Soon I join him and feel the wings of the song lifting me.

I accompany my singing with the tambourine, and the music fills the air with the hope and courage we need so badly at this moment.

"Stop singing, stop singing. My heart is hurting," Mother says, looking at Father and me with a pained face.

"I am sorry, querida," Father says. "It is how I express myself. And Benvenida sings like a nightingale, doesn't she?"

He wipes away the tears from his eyes, and I wipe mine too, though a part of me is happy hearing Father's compliment. Father is a hazan—he sings the songs of our prayers, at synagogue and at home, and he has taught me how to sing too.

I'm not allowed to sing in the synagogue because I'm a girl, but at home I raise my voice and sing proudly.

On the day we leave Toledo, I fear I will be speechless. How will I say goodbye to the only home I've ever known?

3

They Can Take Away My Home but Not My Words

That evening Father's sisters, my aunts Leah and Raquel, come to visit. They are now known by Christian names, Asunción and Juana. They only visit under the cover of night, their faces hidden by their shawls, so as not to raise suspicions that they might be coming to pray or to celebrate a Jewish holiday. And they always come alone, which means I no longer get to spend time with my little cousin Miriam, who is Raquel's daughter. We used to love playing together, hiding and running after each other in the courtyard. How I wish I could just hold her hand for a moment, but I've been told to keep my distance as it could cause her harm to be seen with me.

Now we sit together with my aunts at the kitchen table, and Mother serves the almond marzipan sweets she makes with honey gathered from the hives around Toledo and warm cups of anise brewed with lemon and yet more honey. It is very late, and Isaac and Jacob have already gone to bed, but I am allowed to stay awake so I can help Mother in the kitchen.

Together, my aunts plead with Father. "Samuelico, listen to us. Convert now for the sake of your wife and children. Isn't that wiser than losing everything and taking to the road like a vagabond?"

He responds with fury. "How can you suggest such a thing to me? I may not be a rabbi, but I am a hazan. I am a singer of our sacred prayers. How can I give up the faith of our beloved ancestors? How can I forget the commandments of Moses?"

His sisters whisper, "But haven't you heard that even the great rabbi, Abraham Senior, has converted at the age of eighty? You know you can practice Judaism secretly, like so many do. We still light the candles on Friday night, just for a fleeting moment, to remember we were Jews."

Father shakes his head. "I don't want to snuff out the Shabbat candles. I want their light to shine bright and openly."

The oldest of the two sisters, Tía Asunción, who used to be Tía Leah, speaks firmly. "But, Samuelico, the journey to the seaport is a long one. The heat will be brutal. And how do you know the captains and sailors won't rob you or even kill you at sea? Is it not better to stay here and be safe? Doesn't our faith teach us that life is the holiest thing we possess?"

"There you have a point," Father replies sadly to his sisters. "La vida, life, is everything. I cannot bear the thought of leaving our home here in Toledo, but I also cannot bear the thought of staying and no longer being allowed to keep my faith. That is death to me. I have worn the torn robe of my grief since this day dawned, when I heard the edict of expulsion of the Jews."

No one knows how to reply. We sit in silence. Each and every almond mazapán that Mother shaped into a beautiful half-moon has been eaten, and the warm drinks have all been sipped.

My aunts stand and prepare to leave, adjusting the shawls around their faces again. "Adiós, adiós, adiós," they whisper, only their eyes showing.

Father sighs and replies, "Adiós, hermanicas."

He is tired of battling with them. I feel sad that we were once a united family, and now we will be separated because we no longer share the same faith.

While Father is out during the day with my two brothers, selling our possessions and making plans with other Jews who are leaving, I sit and write. I try to put into words how this most beautiful time of the year, when grapes and olives and figs sprout again, and the trees and flowers bloom and perfume the air, is now heavy with sorrow as we prepare for our departure.

Mother has given me some ink and parchment paper. "Write, Benvenida, write; let your heart speak," she says.

Then she too sits down to write. Our desk is large and edged with a leaf design in inlaid wood. It has been passed down for generations. We look out at the courtyard, the air cool and soft, the hills aglow, the nightingales singing for us.

Mother is always writing letters to her family in Naples, but now her letter is urgent. *We are coming soon, dearest family. We are being expelled from Toledo. Please, please be on the lookout for us.*

She looks up, brushing away a tear. "My beloved parents and brother and sister left for Naples just after you were born, Benvenida. They couldn't bear it here anymore after the king and queen created the Holy Office of the Inquisition to torture the conversos who secretly practiced their Jewish faith."

"Oh, Mother, I fear for Father's sisters and their families."

"I fear for them too, Benvenida. They have to watch their own shadow. Just taking a bath and wearing clean clothes on Friday evening or refusing to eat pork sausages at a neighbor's house could get them reported to the Holy Office. Long ago things were different in Toledo, and Jews and Christians and Muslims lived peacefully here. There were mosques and synagogues and churches. Then King Alfonso conquered the Muslims and built churches on top of the mosques. Soon they will do that with our synagogues—the few that still remain."

"Father had hope that things would get better again."

"Well, your father was wrong! How I wish we had gone to Naples with my family! Now we'll have to fight against our own people to secure passage on one of the ships. It will be very crowded with everyone rushing to the ports at the last minute."

"Mother, crossing the sea scares me."

She gently runs her fingers through my hair. "We will all be together. I will not let you out of my sight for a moment. And we are lucky—in Naples we have family to go to."

My worries disappear for the moment as Mother and I embrace and I smell the rose petals she uses to scent our dresses. Then she glances over at the page where I've written a few more words. "May I read it?"

"Of course," I tell her, but I feel myself blushing as she calmly reads my simple verse aloud.

Nightingales sing
send greetings from those who suffer
to those who are free
tell them the land that was once our home
is now a prison

Mother smiles. "You have a gift, hijica. Keep on writing your poems."

We both settle back into our writing, the light of the afternoon illuminating our words. As I write, I think about how they can take away my home but not my words, the words that form themselves into poems.

I promise myself I will hold on to my language, no matter how far away we go, how many seas we cross, how distant I am from the almond-scented streets of this land. Even at the ends of the earth, I will remember where I came from.

4

We Don't Moan About What We Have Lost

Before we leave, greedy eyes start gazing at our house and don't even pretend to look away. Our house is of modest size and located in the center of the Jewish quarter, which I suppose will no longer be the Jewish quarter after we've all left. What makes it special is the courtyard. From there you can see the golden hills of Toledo and hear the nightingales sing.

The house has been in my mother's family for generations, and the same mezuzah has hung on the doorpost for as long as anyone can remember. But after that horrifying day of the proclamation of the edict of expulsion, Mother takes down our mezuzah, which announces we are Jewish, to bring to our new home.

One afternoon Father opens the door to some men in black cloaks who want to buy our house. They stride from room to room, poking their noses wherever they please, and point to things and ask, "Will that stay? Surely you can't take that chair with you. And the table can't be carried on your back either."

They want to buy the house for a pittance, and Father refuses to accept their miserable offers. Finally, one of them offers a little more and tells Father it is the last offer he will get, so he had better accept it. The man runs his dirty hand over my feather quilt, as if it already belongs to him. After he leaves, I tell Mother I must wash it; I won't be able to sleep otherwise. Though we have little soap, she understands, and we give it a good scrub and let it dry in the courtyard.

Mother sells her earrings and a necklace of pearls that belonged to her great-grandmother. For these precious jewels, she receives only enough to buy the cooking pot we will need on our journey.

"I am sorry, Benvenida," she tells me with tears in her eyes. "I had hoped to pass the family jewelry on to you. But I thought it better to sell it than have it stolen by a robber."

"Do not worry, Mother," I tell her. "You have given me something more precious—the ability to write poems."

We don't moan about what we have lost after we've sold everything—since we can't take it with us, there's no point. Our whole community has lost everything too. We once had ten synagogues in Toledo and five Jewish schools, and soon there will be none. We lived here for hundreds of years, and now we will be nothing but ghosts.

Isaac, who never sheds a tear, cries as he tells us about how the mob ripped the jewel-encrusted velvet covering off our temple's Torah and tossed the holy scroll into the street. The scroll unrolled a bit, but he and Father caught it in time and rushed to roll it up again.

Now Father is determined to make the journey carrying the Torah in his arms. "I wish I could bring every Torah that is being left behind. And the prayer books too. It hurts to think of how they'll be thrown in a pit and burned to ash. At least this one Torah will be safe."

"But it is heavy. How will you manage?" Mother asks.

Isaac says, "I can help carry the Torah."

And Jacob says, "I can also help."

Mother smiles at them. "I always heard my father say the Torah is like a person, so there will be one more person joining us on the journey. Fortunately, not one that needs a plate of food, but one that will be feeding us with wisdom."

5

A Taste of Sweetness as Life Grows Bitter

The kosher butchers have all left town already, so now we eat eggplant with honey and are glad for a taste of sweetness as life grows bitter.

While Mother and I wash and put away the few dishes we haven't yet sold at the market, we hear a faint knock at the door.

It's Tía Raquel—I still can't think of her as Tía Juana—shaking with fear. "The little one wouldn't sleep and insisted on coming with me to say goodbye."

The minute she sees me, little Miriam, now called María, rushes over, and we hug like long-lost sisters.

Mother takes Tía Raquel's trembling hand and leads everyone to the courtyard, where we can see the stars shining in the blue-black sky.

Tía Raquel whispers, "I shudder to think that we may never see each other again."

Miriam looks at me earnestly. "Benvenida, I don't understand why you're leaving."

I wonder how best to explain our situation to my darling little six-year-old cousin. In a world that made sense, I'd be able to watch her grow and continue to give her my clothes when they got too small for me. I'd secretly teach her to write poems, and we could share our dreams.

What can I tell her now that doesn't sound too sad and frightening?

At last I simply say, "We have decided to move to another land." And then, trying my best to seem honest and cheery, I add, "It'll be an adventure, and I'll come back and tell you all about it!"

"Oh! I wish I could travel with you! Will you ride your donkey?" Miriam's eyes get big. "I want to see another land too!"

"But your mother and father need you, precious one," my mother says.

"They can come with us!" Miriam says.

Tía Raquel sighs. "We will stay here in Toledo, mi niña, so when Benvenida returns, she will have a place to stay."

"So when you come back, I'll see you more!" Miriam flings her arms around my neck with such affection I have to struggle not to cry.

"The sky is so pretty now. Let's count the stars," I say.

This makes Miriam giggle. "There are too many! But I am good at counting!"

While Miriam is counting, I hear Tía Raquel whisper to my father. "When I am in church, reciting the rosary, I still hear the Hebrew prayers in my ears. I hear the blast of the shofar. Then I look above and see angels and the spirits of Mother and Father weeping."

Father wraps an arm around her shoulder. "This is a difficult time, hermanica, and we each made the best choice we could. I am sure Mother and Father are blessing you from on high."

Miriam had been listening. "I hear the shofar and see the angels too! They are beautiful, with rosy faces, like the ones smiling at the Virgin in the church."

I start to smile at how Miriam is confusing the two religions, until I see the terror in Tía Raquel's eyes and know how careful she has to be so her child won't say anything that could get them reported to the Inquisition.

Tía Raquel stands and reaches for Miriam's hand. "Time to go, María. Say goodbye to your cousin."

Miriam holds on to me, not wanting to let go—and I don't want to let go either.

"Be a good girl, my darling cousin. Listen to your mother," I say. "Next time I see you, we will sing happy songs and play the tambourine."

Her eyes light up. "Really?"

I nod and we hug again, more tightly this time.

Tía Raquel draws the shawl carefully around her face and wraps Miriam in a smaller shawl.

"Adiós," they say.

That word never sounded so sad.

After they leave, I imagine little Miriam years from now, trying to remember me, her cousin who left. She will never know that after she said adiós, I gazed up at the sky and asked, *Will there be a next time?* And I received no answer.

I catch a whiff of mazapán de almendra, the almond marzipan of this land, and think of all I will miss.

That night I write a few words of goodbye to Toledo. I walk out into the courtyard, and when my eyes adjust to the darkness, I hide the parchment deep in one of the crevices in the wall surrounding our house. Maybe someone will read it one day and remember I lived here. And if the parchment is never found, at least some of my words will stay in Toledo.

6

Singing, We Leave Toledo

At the crack of dawn, I hear the nightingales sing. *Adiós, adiós,* they seem to say as I look out at the sun rising over the golden hills of Toledo.

The day has finally come when we can no longer put off leaving.

Mother tried to get Father to leave sooner, but he was holding out hope that the edict of expulsion might be revoked. Mother assured him that was not going to happen, but still Father kept delaying our departure, until we were among the very last to leave. Until only a few days remained before Jews who stayed would be hanged.

We all take one last look at our home, and then Father closes our front door and puts the key inside his robe.

Mother asks, "You are taking the key, Samuelico? What for?"

He responds, "Let the man who bought it for a pittance break the door open if he wants our house so badly. It will always be ours whether we're here or not. And who's to say we won't return one day?"

She gives him a sympathetic look but says nothing more.

Father brushes away his tears and stands close to my brothers and me. "Children, I bless you in the name of El Dio that we make the journey safely. Now let's walk down the hill with our heads tall. Remember, look ahead. Don't look back, or you will turn to salt."

Father lifts the Torah onto his shoulder, preparing to carry it on our long journey to Valencia, the city where we plan to board a ship to Naples.

It pains me to see the scroll missing its beautiful covering of velvet cloth and gemstones. It's wrong for our sacred Torah to be exposed to the sun and heat of a July morning, so I take my shawl out of the small bag that I packed with some clothing and parchment and pens. The shawl's embroidered with red and pink roses and was a gift for my twelfth birthday. I hand it to Father and say, "I know this is only a shawl, but if you wish to cover the Torah with it, I would be honored."

And Father immediately replies, "I accept your gift, Benvenida. What a kind thought."

He wraps my shawl around the Torah scroll, and we begin our march.

My mother rides our donkey, and my brothers, Isaac and Jacob, carry our provisions—bread and cheese, eggplant empanadillas, roasted eggs, olives cured in salt, dried figs, almonds, and walnuts—and our few belongings.

I have my poems sewn into the hem of my dress, and I

know Mother is carrying a purse with coins hidden inside her robe.

We are not alone. As we pass through the stone walls of the town, all the last Jews departing form a procession so large we are a river of people. Tailors, leather workers, cobblers, tanners, weavers, spice dealers, peddlers, merchants, silversmiths, goldsmiths—a whole wonderful community that lived and worked together and flourished—are being forced to leave. Children and elders, on foot or riding donkeys or being pulled along on carts, all look ahead; none look back. We wear the yellow-and-red badges on our clothes that brand us as Jews. We are the ones who won't hide. The ones who have lost everything except our faith.

Some Christians—old and new—with whom we once shared the town gawk at us. A few shout, "Leave, leave! ¡Fuera, fuera! Leave and never return!"

It hurts to hear those words, and it's hard to hold my head high. I feel myself crumpling inside and out, like a withering rose. Then I glance to the side and see my friends, Susanah and Deborah, standing hand in hand. We haven't spoken in over a year, ever since their families converted, but now I feel an urge to wish them well.

"¡Vida larga y mazal bueno!" I call out, wishing them a long life and good luck.

They seem to be waving to me, and just as I raise my arm to wave back, I see they are holding stones in their hands, which they throw at us!

One almost hits me, and when Father sees this he says, "Benvenida, don't cry. Bring out your tambourine, and we'll sing."

When we begin to sing, a silence seems to fall upon the world. Even the nightingales listen. Soon all those who are leaving sing with us:

> *¿Por qué no cantas, galana?*
> *¿Por qué no cantas, la bella?*
> *Ay, galana y bella ...*
> *—Ni canto, ni cantaré,*
> *que mi amor está en la guerra ...*
>
> *Why don't you sing, elegant girl?*
> *Why don't you sing, beautiful one?*
> *Ay, you who are elegant and beautiful ...*
> *—I don't sing, I won't sing,*
> *while my love is away in the war ...*

Singing, we leave Toledo, crossing the bridge across the Río Tajo, then going past the vineyards and olive groves, and take to the road, not knowing what dangers might await us.

7

Sleep, Sleep, Without Fear and Pain

We march along the flat plain, and Father struggles under the weight of the Torah. My brothers walk on either side of Father. Every so often, he leans against Isaac, who is already taller than him, to catch his breath. Mother stays on the donkey, and I guide her forward. I am wearing my lightest muslin dress and robe, but all clothing feels heavy in the summer heat. Sweat drips down my back. Blisters form on my feet.

By midday, the heat is unbearable. We are thirsty, hungry, tired. The procession stops, though a few of the more robust among us keep on marching ahead, hoping to reach Valencia first and find a ship going to Naples or any other land that will take them. Fortunately, two men who know the route agree to stay with us to the very end and serve as our guides.

We sit with the other families in the shade of some trees on the side of the road. Mother takes out the roasted eggs, which need to be eaten soonest, and we eat them slowly, savoring each bite. Father sings the blessings of gratitude after our meal, and my brothers and other men sing with him.

> *Bendigamos al Altisímo, al Señor que nos crió.*
> *Démosle agradecimiento por los bienes que nos dio.*

> *Let us bless the one on high, the Lord who created us.*
> *Let us give him thanks for the good things he has given us.*

Small children run around the trees in circles until they're dizzy, and babies cry until they're fed by their tired mothers. Elders sigh and look for El Dio in the sky and ask for strength.

There's a pregnant woman next to us, and she lies on a blanket, rubbing her belly while her husband sits at her side. She smiles at me and says her name is Naomi and lets me feel how the baby is moving around inside her. In a soft voice, I sing the lullaby Father sings to me:

> *Durme, durme, querida hijica*
> *Durme, durme, sin ansia y dolor*
> *Cierra tus chicos ojicos*
> *Durme, durme, con sabor*

> *Sleep, sleep, dear daughter*
> *Sleep, sleep, without fear and pain*
> *Close your little eyes*
> *Sleep, sleep, with joy*

We have many days of walking ahead, so no one takes a siesta. We just rest for a bit before gathering our things and heading back on the road.

The afternoon sun is intense, and I slip into a daze, dreaming of cool water in which to bathe. At home I might be sitting at the desk in our peaceful house, reading or writing with Mother. I miss our old life so much already! But then I touch the hem of my dress and know my poems are with me. One day I will sit somewhere again and write.

Just before dusk, we reach a small town called La Mora. A few humble huts stand near the entrance to the town. Farmers and shepherds gather the sheep and goats to bring them to the barns, where they will be safe for the night.

A man with ruddy cheeks approaches our group and says, "We thought all the Jews had left by now. We have seen many take this road."

Father tells him that we are the last group to leave from Toledo, so after us there won't be many others passing through. He asks the man if we can all spend the night in the fields.

"You can stay," the man says. "And we can give you water and wine and milk for the children. We won't charge you too much." He smiles and points at me. "That beautiful maiden, if she wants a bed to sleep in, she can have mine."

Father and Mother gasp. My brothers draw closer, and I want to disappear.

"Our daughter will stay with us," Father responds.

"As you wish." The man laughs at my embarrassment.

I don't raise my eyes until the man leaves.

Our group walks out into the field, and we spread our blankets on the meadows where the sheep and goats graze during the day. The men bring the water and wine and milk, and we wash our hands and drink and eat from our provisions.

We have many more days ahead on our journey, so as soon as the sun sets we try to sleep.

I know Mother is worried because she takes my hand in hers and won't let go. She falls asleep, still holding on, and I stay awake.

The coolness I longed for earlier arrives with the night, as does the howling of wolves in the distance. Shivering in the darkness, I huddle closer to Mother and listen to her gentle breathing. Father sleeps nearby with his arms wrapped around the Torah, and my brothers sleep on either side of him.

All around me the last Jews of Toledo sleep under the stars, and I pray for our safety.

8

She Will Be Called Preciada

Days merge together, and then it is dawn again, the time when I most want to sleep. I know we're lucky that people let us sleep in their fields, but sleeping on the hard ground brings no real rest.

We set off, passing through dry and barren hills. I'm still groggy, but a rage is starting to build in me. I recall the morning I heard the edict of expulsion and how I didn't understand what it meant. Now I can feel in my bones the meaning of that ugly word, *expulsion*.

Why have we been thrown out of our homes and made to live like wild beasts? Even sheep and goats have barns to sleep in to protect them from the cold and the wolves.

Anger pulses through my veins as the morning sun gets higher, and I walk with greater determination, pulling the donkey and Mother along with me.

"Slow down!" Isaac yells. "Don't use up your energy! And don't tire the donkey, or it will stop and refuse to move!"

I turn and wait for Father and my brothers to catch up.

Behind them I see elders stopping to catch their breath

and babies crying to be fed, but their mothers keep moving forward. Children complain, and their parents beg them to walk a little more, just a little more.

I feel the most pity for Naomi, holding her heavy belly as she hobbles along on swollen feet. Several of us have offered her our donkeys, but she stubbornly says she wants to walk.

We are just over forty people, now that so many who started the journey with us have gone ahead of our slow group.

After a short break for water, we walk for several hours more in the burning light of the sun. There is hardly any shade on this road, just field after field of tall, dry grass growing in clumps. I tell Father that I don't like the looks of this grass with blades so sharp they might cut your hand if you dare to pull on them.

"This is esparto," Father says. "It is rough but useful. See the rope tying our things to the donkey's back? That is esparto. See Naomi's espadrille sandals? Esparto. The basket we use to carry our bread, that's esparto too. Even the roughest material can be turned into beautiful and useful things by one who knows how to work it."

And then Naomi begins to moan. She clasps her husband Simón's elbow and says she can go no farther. The baby is about to be born.

"Looks like there's a village up ahead," someone says. "We can stop there for Naomi."

As Naomi collapses to the ground, the women rush to

create a nest of blankets for her to rest on. She lies down, rocking from side to side.

Mother's grandmother was a midwife, and Mother watched her deliver babies, so she knows what to do. She crouches next to Naomi and holds her hand and tells her to not be afraid of the pain.

Suddenly two men from the village appear. They carry swords and wear large crosses around their necks. They stare at our red-and-yellow badges marking us as Jewish. They see the women encircling Naomi, who's still holding on to Mother for support.

"This is the village of El Romeral," the taller man says. "No Jew has ever lived here, and we do not wish you to stop here. Pack your things and go peacefully, or blood will be shed."

The shorter man says, "We fought to rid Granada of the Moors, and we are ready to fight to rid Castile of the Jews."

Father bows respectfully. "We are making our way to the seaport of Valencia, leaving this land as the king and queen, Our Majesties, have ordered. We have only stopped here because a baby is about to be born. We will go as soon as we can; I give you my word."

The taller man shakes his head. "A baby born in El Romeral must be baptized as a Christian. We will call upon the priest immediately."

From the women's circle comes the voice of Naomi. "No! My baby shall not be baptized!"

The shorter man points his sword at Father. "Then leave,

I say! Leave now or you will regret setting foot on this soil."

With difficulty, Naomi rises and says, "Let's go. My sweet baby will wait a little longer."

Mother and Simón help Naomi onto our donkey, and we march ahead, crossing through low hills, until we see another town on the horizon.

Soon Naomi announces, "The baby is coming!"

Once again we find Naomi a spot off the side of the road, this time where there's a bit of shade. Mother sits beside her, and the other women encircle Naomi, holding up their blankets to create a tent for some privacy.

Simón paces nervously, and the men gather around him, praying and trying to offer comfort.

It isn't long before the baby is born. Mother catches her—a girl, with a full head of dark hair and a strong set of lungs.

"¡Es una niña!" everyone repeats.

"She will be called Preciada," Naomi says. "For she is precious."

Acting as if we're in the synagogue rather than on the side of the road, Father sings a few prayers in honor of the newborn girl. Then he blesses Naomi and Simón. He smiles, looking around at our group. "El Dio allows us these moments of happiness to lift our spirits, even as we suffer through the sorrow of departure."

Young and old join hands and dance and stomp on the esparto grass to create a smooth bed for everyone, and we lay our blankets down.

My brothers and several other young men walk to the

town and return with water, bread, cheese, milk, and wine. Father sings the blessings. We eat and drink with gratitude, mothers at last tending to the babies, the elders sinking fast into sleep, hugging the earth.

Soon all are asleep, except for Father, who is still sitting up. I watch him gaze at the stars, his lips moving quietly in prayer.

"Father, is everything all right?" I whisper.

"Dulce Benvenida, why are you awake now?"

"I can't sleep, Father. I hear the wolves howling."

"But you must sleep, hijica. Close your eyes, and I will sing to you."

"Durme, durme, sin ansia y dolor," he begins softly.

Suddenly he stops and holds his hand to his heart.

"Father, what is wrong?"

"Nothing, hijica. I'm sure it is the emotion of leaving our home. At night, the pain and the sadness catch up with me."

"I am sorry, Father. Soon we will be in Valencia and find a ship and start a new life."

"Of course we will!" He again softly sings:

Sleep, sleep, dear daughter
Sleep, sleep, without fear and pain . . .

He keeps singing until I fall asleep, his voice as soothing as it has been since the day I took my first breath.

9

The Forest

The next morning a local priest appears, accompanied by some townspeople. He shrewdly takes note of the declining health of the elders and says, "Do not suffer anymore. Those of you who are infirm, stay and we will care for you. All you need do is accept the Cross, and our doctor will tend to your health until your final days. Whatever silver coins you carry in your purse will be sufficient. We ask nothing more than that you profess a sincere faith and cast aside your Jewish ways once and for all." He looks at the miserable elders, many of whose heads are bowed in shame, and says, "Who is ready to accept baptism?"

One of the trembling elders says, "I will accept baptism. I do not want to be a burden to my family any longer."

His children and grandchildren weep, but they let him go. "Be well—it is better that you live as a Christian than that you die as a Jew in the wilderness, eaten by wolves and vultures," his daughter says.

Two more elders follow. "Forgive us," one of them says.

"It is better that we convert so you don't have to bury us on the roadside."

We watch as these elders, once proud Jews, walk slowly behind the priest, wanting nothing but a bowl of soup and a bed after the miserable time on the road.

One elder stays put, waiting for the others to be out of earshot, and declares, "I would rather die than convert."

We go on, praying that one day soon the wide blue sea will shine on the horizon.

But that day seems not to want to arrive, and the journey has begun to take its toll on all of us.

Father continues to carry the Torah wrapped in my shawl, but now the weight is becoming too much for him. He gasps for breath and limps. Isaac gently asks if he can have the honor of carrying the Torah for a while, and Father passes it to him. Then Jacob hooks arms with Father, and I see how Father leans into Jacob as if carrying his own weight has also become difficult.

Mother shakes her head and gives me a tired smile. I reach and embrace her, feeling her sweat, longing for the days when she smelled of rose petals.

I look out at our group and see a procession of broken people—unwashed, our hair caked with dirt, our clothes torn, open wounds on our feet, losing faith in everything we once held dear.

The road gets rougher. And when we reach a dense forest of trees, so tall they seem to reach the sky, a few of our fellow travelers balk. "Why do you want to take us into these dark woods?" they ask angrily. "There might be wild animals, and we'll be eaten alive!"

But the men who are familiar with the route assure us this is the way and that on the other side we will find a small inn run by a kind man. The dream of a good meal and a night of rest gives us the strength to walk through the forest.

At last, we find the cool shade we longed for on our sweltering journey. But the thick roots of the trees have come up from the earth and created clumps along the path, making it difficult to walk. Mother and others who are riding on donkeys must step down and cajole the donkeys to keep moving, and it's almost impossible to maneuver the carts.

Only Naomi seems not to worry. She leans against a tree, nursing her baby. I recall the words that Father used to sing at the synagogue at the naming ceremony for girls, and I sing them to Preciada:

> *Show me your face*
> *let me hear your voice*
> *for your voice is sweet*
> *and your face is lovely . . .*

Father turns and smiles. "You remember, Benvenida, you remember." And tears come to his eyes. "Sing, hijica, keep singing."

And then I think about the song I've heard since I was

little, about a young girl who is stuck in a tall tower at sea, and she lifts her voice and sings to the sailors who pass by in their ships. *I am here, I am alive, listen to me*, she croons, as much to herself as to them. I pull out my tambourine and sing:

> *En la mar hay una torre,*
> *en la torre una ventana,*
> *en la ventana una hija*
> *que a los marineros llama.*
>
> *In the sea there is a tower,*
> *in the tower there is a window,*
> *at the window a daughter*
> *who calls to the sailors.*

Everyone listens. The music rises into the air with the wings of a nightingale and carries us forward, just when it seems we cannot take another step.

A flicker of the setting sun appears through the leaves of the trees behind us. Ahead, through a gap in the treetops, we catch a glimpse of clouds, pink and gray in the fading twilight. We walk toward the gap and find our way out of the forest.

10

Adiós, Amina, Adiós

It isn't long before we come upon the inn we've heard about, where a man who goes by the nickname El Moro lives with his family. We learn that El Moro was a Muslim who lived by the sea in Valencia, then moved north and converted to Christianity. Everyone still knows him as El Moro, and now he and his wife and their seven children run the inn. They know we're Jews, yet they greet us kindly and don't try to convert us.

"Come in, come in," they say. "You must be tired from your journey. Now you can rest for a couple of nights and get your strength back."

Even though the inn is small, it has many rooms, enough for all of us to stay indoors.

They give us cool water to bathe in, scented with rose petals. That makes Mother so happy. "Gracias, gracias, gracias," she repeats.

After we've bathed and tended to our blisters and wounds, we feel like ourselves again. It is the eve of

Shabbat, and we feel fortunate to be able to celebrate our day of rest with hope and joy.

We are served cheese and eggs and bread and sweet cakes, made with walnuts and honey. Everything tastes like manna from the sky.

Father sings the prayers of gratitude after the meal, and we listen with tears in our eyes.

> *Pues comimos y bebimos alegremente; su merced nunca nos faltó . . .*
> *For we have eaten and drunk with joy; his mercy has never left us . . .*

Then he says, "Let's not cry. The sea is closer to us now. We will be on our way before we know it. El Dio has not forgotten us."

That night, we sleep in straw beds. I sleep next to Mother and happily breathe in the scent of rose petals. It is peaceful here, and I am no longer afraid. I fall asleep as soon as I close my eyes.

When I awake the next morning, the sun is high in the sky. Mother let me rest. I get up to explore and find Mother in a room with a group of women, sharing stories. Most of the men have gathered in another room to pray. From the door, I see Father chanting from the Torah, being careful not to touch the Hebrew words with his fingers, since the silver yad, the pointer, was stolen in Toledo.

Outside, the children run and play. It feels good to hear their laughter. I watch, wishing I could join them, but I'm not a little child anymore.

When I step away from the children, I see one of the daughters of El Moro, who looks to be my age. She smiles at me, and I say, "I am Benvenida."

"I am Amina," she answers.

"It is so nice here, I wish we could stay."

"Why can't you stay?"

"We are Jews," I tell her. "The king and queen do not want us to live in this land anymore."

"I am sorry," Amina replies. She comes closer and whispers, "My father says, before I was born, he and my mother were Muslim. But now they're Christian. We don't eat pork, but they have a ham hanging from the window so nobody will think badly of us. And sometimes they speak Arabic. They teach us some, but secretly, since we're only supposed to speak Spanish in this land."

"I know a few words of Arabic," I tell Amina. "There's a poet from long ago whose work I love." I repeat the Arabic words from Qasmuna. "'I'm dark-eyed just like you, and lonely.'"

Amina's eyes brighten. "You do know Arabic! And I often feel the same way as the poet."

"Me too," I tell her. "I had two good friends in Toledo, but they stopped speaking to me after they converted. Susanah and Deborah were their names. We did everything together when we were little. But when we left Toledo, they threw stones at us."

Amina can't believe that girls who used to be my friends would do such a cruel thing. She takes my hand, and for the rest of our time at the inn we are inseparable.

We daydream that she hides me in one of the rooms of the inn and I get to stay. We daydream that she'll leave with me and we'll cross the sea together and find out what is on the other side.

The next day, I am up at dawn with my family and our people. We have been restored and feel ready for the last couple of days of the journey.

As our procession departs, El Moro and his wife and seven children wave goodbye.

"Buen viaje," they call.

I see Amina wipe the tears from her eyes with her handkerchief, and I feel bad that such fine fabric is being filled with sorrow, hers and mine.

"Adiós, Amina, adiós," I say.

"Adiós, Benvenida, adiós," she replies. Then she comes over and slips her handkerchief into my palm. "Take this, so you'll remember the friend in Venta del Moro who cried for you."

Holding the wet handkerchief, I set off, grateful to know I still have a friend in the land where I was born.

11

Open a Road Through the Sea

With our renewed strength we move at a faster pace. But Father struggles to keep up. When Mother asks if he wants to ride on the donkey, he refuses. But he lets Isaac continue to carry the Torah and doesn't let go of Jacob's arm the rest of the way. Several times, Father turns to me and says, "Play your tambourine, Benvenida." I shake out a tune, and that seems to make the journey easier for him.

Soon the air smells and tastes different. We're finally approaching the coast!

There is an old castle on a hill, in ruins, and Father says it has probably been there since the days when the Moors ruled. I think of Amina and her family secretly speaking Arabic. I wonder if anything will be left of our temples, language, and customs? Will it all disappear forever once we're gone? Will our presence here in this land only be spoken about in secret?

After circling around the hills, we find ourselves coming down a long slope. There is a town nearby called Siete Aguas, and I try to imagine what seven waters the town is named for. I am sure that the springs gush with water, and creeks and rivers are flowing everywhere, as the landscape has turned the brightest green.

Those who know the route say we can make it to the coast in a day or two if we leave early in the morning and walk at a steady pace. The route will be downhill now on a broad, smooth path, the easiest we have found in our journey.

But watching Father struggle to breathe, I worry. He needs to rest, and the only accommodation we can find for the night is a stretch of green meadow, where the grass fortunately is soft. Everyone sets up their blankets for what we pray is our last night of sleep outdoors.

It takes another day, and another day, another night and another night, until mercifully we arrive. Father insists on carrying the Torah as we descend the path to the sea. Hope must have given him a burst of energy as he's able to keep up with the group.

Once we come closer to the port, seagulls flying above us, flapping their wings, we notice the huge numbers of homeless outcasts like ourselves.

I knew other Jews would be seeking passage on the ships, but I didn't expect the port to be crowded from end to end. Only a few days remain before all the Jews in the kingdom who haven't converted have to leave—or else they will be hanged.

Too many, like us, have delayed their departure until the bitter end.

Soon everyone in our group from Toledo is saying goodbye and wishing one another a safe journey.

Before we part ways, my father recites a prayer that we all repeat:

Show us mercy.
Show us a miracle.
Open a road through the sea.
Let us again be free.

I hug Naomi and cuddle with Preciada, not wanting to let her go. Simón smiles and says, "Don't worry, Benvenida. I will take good care of them."

As they rush off, I wave and call out, "Maybe a miracle will happen, and we will meet again someday!"

And Naomi calls back, "Let's hope so! I haven't lost faith in miracles yet!"

12

Pray Our Broken Souls Will Heal

The sun is lost in the fog as we push our way closer to the docks to find out which ships are going where and which still have room for passengers.

I squint at the ships anchored in the harbor, their flags furled, their hulls bobbing in the sea's waves.

It strikes me that there are too few ships for the many Jews who need to depart. How will all of us ever leave in time?

"Too windy to travel," a sailor announces, and the news spreads quickly through the crowd that no ships will sail today.

Exhausted by the journey, we take this news of the delay badly. Mother and Father and Isaac and Jacob and I fall upon one another and weep.

Isaac is the first to regain his composure. Being the eldest, he always looks out for the family. He clears his throat and says, "We will try again tomorrow. And if there's not enough room for all of us on the ship, I shall wait or find another seaport."

Then Jacob, never wanting to be seen as the helpless little brother, chimes in, "No, Isaac, let it be me who stays behind. I am swifter than you, and I will manage on my own."

Mother looks at them both and says, "Stop speaking such terrible words, boys! They are like a dagger in my heart. We will all leave together, or we won't leave at all!"

Father nods and says, "Your mother is right. We must never lose our faith in El Dio. We will cross the sea together."

Since we are fortunate enough to be in a town with lots of inns, we set off to find one. The crowded streets reek of rotten fish, and it pains me to see Father limping again. He leans against Jacob, who carries the Torah for him, while Isaac gently pulls Mother along on the donkey. She stares ahead in a haze of exhaustion.

How cruel this journey has been. Were Father's sisters, Leah and Raquel, right? It would have been so much easier to have converted and stayed in Toledo. But I try to erase these thoughts from my mind and pray our broken souls will heal when we arrive in a new land.

We find the row of inns that serve the vast numbers of Jews looking for shelter at the seaport before their departure. "¡Aquí, aquí!" shout the innkeepers, competing with one another to get our attention, each claiming their rates are cheaper.

Father chooses the innkeeper who sits on a stool in front of his inn. He doesn't say a word but nods politely as we approach.

"Come inside. You must be tired from the heat," the innkeeper says, and brings us into a quiet room that smells soothingly of lavender.

Father settles on a price with the innkeeper, and soon the innkeeper's wife appears with cool juice for us to drink.

We're invited to rest in the courtyard. It has a gurgling fountain in the center. Lemon and orange trees have been planted in large clay pots on each corner, and flowering bushes perfume the air. Doves coo in a dovecote.

I want to stay here forever.

"It is crowded at the harbor," Father says. "How will all of us depart as we've been ordered to in the next few days?"

The innkeeper gazes at us with pity. "Many won't find a ship in time and might choose death rather than convert. Would you not prefer to convert and stay?"

Father replies, "We have come all the way from Toledo, without looking back. Our minds are made up."

"I understand," the innkeeper says. "I am a converso. Not long ago I too was a Jew; my wife as well. I used to be a merchant. I have traveled far and wide on many vessels. You must be careful about which ship you board. Some sailors will steal from you, and unless you can afford a closed cabin, you will be crammed onto a filthy deck with far too many seasick people."

"Thank you for the warning," Father replies.

"Baruch Hashem," the innkeeper says with a sad smile.

Father looks at him in surprise.

"You see? I have not forgotten how to say 'blessed is God' in Hebrew. Now tell me: What is your destination?"

"Naples," Father tells him.

"Very well. I believe there is a ship leaving for Naples the day after tomorrow—I will help you arrange passage. I can buy your donkey too, if you wish for me to give you more coins for the journey ahead."

Father rises and holds out his hand to the innkeeper. "I will never forget your kindness."

In the night I toss and turn, crying into Amina's handkerchief, asking how it is that we are leaving our beloved land. How is it that we have no home any longer?

I think of the song Father taught me, of the maiden in the sea, in the tower, calling out to the sailors. That is how I feel, lost at sea, though I'm still on dry land. But I pray all will be well. And then I let the cooing doves sing me to sleep.

13

Remember, Hijica, Live the Truth of Who You Are

Thanks to the innkeeper's help, on the day promised we are aboard a ship in a closed cabin traveling to Naples.

Mother and Father have spent almost all their coins to pay for this luxury. We hope Mother's family has received her letters telling them we are on the way, and they will take us in until Father can work again and be responsible for us.

As we leave the harbor, Father says a prayer for crossing the sea:

> *May it be your will, the Almighty, the Great, the Powerful, and the Awesome*
> *That you calm the ocean from its rage and still its waves*
> *That you quickly guide us to our desired destination . . .*

I imagine the world I know fading away. "Adiós, adiós, adiós," I whisper.

The Mediterranean Sea is calm as our ship slides slowly

away from the port as in a dream. The water is a breathtaking shade of turquoise, like nothing I've ever seen. Amid the sorrow of our departure, I allow myself to savor its beauty and dare to imagine for a moment that I am an explorer going in search of new lands. I'm hoping my future will be filled with new adventures and all our suffering will be left behind.

Above our deck, people move back and forth endlessly, the sound of their steps echoing in our ears. But we are relieved not to have to walk anywhere, to just sit and wait.

"We will be there soon," Father says. "I know we are ready to start a new life."

Then, as one day and another and another pass, we are all stricken with seasickness and grow weak from vomiting and dizzy spells. Father sleeps through the day and lies awake at night, tossing and turning, muttering prayers to El Dio, who seems not to be listening.

Once I am feeling hungry again, I discover there is little food on the ship, aside from moldy bread and the pork sausages we can't eat. We carefully ration the biscuits, cheese, and dried figs we have brought for the voyage, hoping they will last us. Isaac, always the responsible older brother, gives Jacob and me a little extra of his portion, and we accept those morsels gratefully.

Mother doesn't let me out of her sight and forbids me to leave our cabin, but the stink and the darkness are awful, and one morning I beg her to let me step out for some fresh air.

"Go with Isaac and Jacob," she says. "And be fast."

We climb to the main deck and look out at the sea, where choppy waves rise up, menacing as swords. Around us are other people who smell, as we do, of salt, sweat, and vomit. I inhale a breath of air, but it doesn't make me feel that much better—and it's not worth risking Mother's nerves by staying outside too long, so we return to our cabin.

Father's still sleeping, and Mother's pacing anxiously. "Dear children, I know you weren't gone very long, but still I couldn't stay calm without you."

After that, I stay in the cabin. I am pained to see Father's condition worsen as he drifts in and out of sleep. Mother and I tend to him, washing his face with cool water, and Isaac and Jacob sit by his side, praying.

One evening Father awakens and asks to hold the Torah in his arms. He keeps it close the whole night, grasping it with the little strength he has left.

The following day, he slowly says his goodbyes.

To Isaac and Jacob, he says, "My sons, I am not going to make it. Take care of the family and the Torah."

To Mother, he says, "Courage, my dear wife. Know that I admire you for your great wisdom and will love you always."

I want to say, *Oh dearest Father, you should have listened to your sisters. They will be so heartbroken. If we'd done what they asked, we'd still be home.* But I don't want to hurt him; he is suffering enough.

Somehow Father reads my mind, and he says, "I have no

regrets, Benvenida, and you shouldn't either. I am grateful I brought you to the sea. I won't be with you when you set foot in the new land, but I've not lost faith in El Dio. I know El Dio will protect you. Remember, hijica, always live the truth of who you are, not the falsehood that others may wish to force upon you."

Father knows it is the Ninth of Av—the day we remember the destruction of the two holy temples of Jerusalem. He closes his eyes, and with his last breath, he says, "I am dying on the saddest day of the year. This is the will of El Dio, and I go in peace."

Mother begs the captain to let us keep Father's body on board until we land, so that we can bury him, but the captain says the dead cannot remain aboard the ship. So Isaac and Jacob carry Father up to the deck, and then we recite the Kaddish, the prayer for the dead.

*May there be abundant peace from heaven
and life, for us, and for all Israel
and say amen.*

In a whisper, Father is released to the sea. He will rest until the end of time in the watery grave that lies between the land we have left and the land we will soon know.

The sea, the sea . . .

The sea will always remind me of Father.

14

I Carry My Tambourine

Our ship finally anchors in Naples and only four of us disembark.

How I wish Father had lived to see this bustling port city. Valencia is just a little village compared to Naples, a city that rises majestically along the edge of the sea. Never have I seen so many elegant houses, castles, and churches arranged like a painting on the horizon.

"There's a volcano out there too," Isaac says, "called Mount Vesuvius."

"But don't worry, it won't erupt again," Jacob jokes. "At least not while we're here!"

Ships sway at the dock, so many I can't count them all. They disgorge numerous goods carried away on the backs of men and brought to horse-drawn carriages waiting to transport them to the city.

"Move along, don't dawdle here," one of the sailors from our ship says, shooing us away as we gaze around with amazement and fear and try to gather our strength. We are feeling weak from the loss of Father. He would have uttered a prayer and guided us forward.

Jacob carries the Torah and Isaac holds on to Mother as we leave the harbor. I carry my tambourine—but for what reason I don't know, since I can't imagine singing again. And I still have Amina's tear-stained handkerchief.

For a while we wander along unfamiliar streets, hearing words in Neapolitan, a language we can almost understand. All Mother knows, from the letters she's received from her family, is that they live near the harbor, next to a plaza with a large market, in a neighborhood where many Jews have settled in recent years.

Passing a cluster of houses made from the gray stone of the region, we come upon several children who are speaking our language and playing in the street. What a joyous sight!

We ask them where the family of printers lives, and right away they point to the top of the street.

As we approach the front door, Mother calls out, "Madre, Padre, hermana, hermano, hemos llegado."

The door flies open, and a woman who must be our grandmother runs out and takes Mother into her arms, saying, "Hijica, hijica, you are here!"

She is followed by a man who must be our grandfather. He looks at Mother as if he hardly recognizes her.

Mother says, "Yes, Padre, it is me. But I am a shadow of who I was. I have lost my home. I have lost my husband—my dear beloved Samuelico just died at sea." And she breaks into tears and can say nothing else, while both her parents hug her.

Then Grandfather steps over to us.

"You must be Isaac, the eldest?" Grandfather asks.

"I am," he responds.

"And you are Jacob," Grandfather continues.

"I am," he responds.

"You, mi niña, are Benvenida," Grandfather then says.

"I am," I say.

Grandmother, still holding Mother in her arms, says, "Let us go inside—your sister and brother will be so happy to see you. We'll get you settled. You must eat and rest."

We kiss the mezuzah that is on the doorpost, not hidden, and we enter their house, where we are greeted by my mother's sister and brother—Tía Mazal and Tío Yehuda.

"I see you have brought a Torah all the way from Toledo," says Tío Yehuda.

Jacob replies, "Yes, Father carried it most of the way."

"He will be blessed in heaven for such a good deed," Grandfather pronounces. He then adds, "I must say that is an unusual vestido for the Torah."

Isaac explains. "The velvet mantles were taken from all the Torahs in Toledo. This covering is a shawl that belongs to Benvenida. She offered it so the Torah wouldn't be uncovered while we carried it from place to place."

"That was a fine thing to do, querida Benvenida," Grandfather says, smiling.

But then Tía Mazal looks at me and frowns. "What

happened to your dress, Benvenida? I will have to teach you how to sew a hem properly."

I look down and notice that my hem has bunched up on one side and is no longer smooth. In time, I will tell her about the poems hidden inside the seams of my dress, but now I just nod and smile.

They lead us to a room filled with papers and inks and a printing machine.

"Is this where you make the books?" I ask my uncle. I can't hold back my excitement.

"Yes, Benvenida. I will show you after you have rested," Tío Yehuda replies, smiling.

"And I am ready to work," Isaac says.

"As am I," Jacob adds.

"Thank you, dear nephews, we need more hands." Tío Yehuda smiles again.

"But now you must bathe," Tía Mazal says. "And then we will eat."

There is a spare room for my brothers, and Mother and I will share a room with Tía Mazal. It is a spacious house, but what I like best is the scent of ink and paper and books filling the air with hopefulness.

They give us copper basins filled with fresh water. After we wash, we find clean clothes set out for us on our beds.

When we sit down to eat, everything tastes as delicious as it had in Toledo in the days when we were happy, before the expulsion.

"As we left Toledo, Father told me to play the tambourine

and sing," I tell our family. "Even though we are mourning the loss of Father, I think Father would want me to sing for you." And playing on my tambourine, I sing:

> ¿Por qué no cantas, galana?
> ¿Por qué no cantas, la bella?

Grandfather says, "You sing like a nightingale, dear child."

"That was what Father used to say." I try not to cry when I hear myself say "used to," but the tears come anyway.

"Well, your father was right," Grandfather says, and gives me a hug.

Mother tells the story of our journey, and then we all cry and hold our hands to our hearts.

"What you have gone through to find freedom!" Grandmother says.

"I wish we had come sooner." Mother sighs. "You were right to leave before things became so frightening."

"It has been good here until now," Tío Yehuda says. "But we might have to leave Naples before too long. Many suffer from hunger, Jewish and Christian. The other day, a Jewish peddler sold his son into slavery to feed the rest of his family."

"Cholera is spreading through the region," Tía Mazal adds. "And Christians blame Jews whenever there is illness."

Mother asks, "Where would you go then?"

Tío Yehuda replies, "We have heard that the Turkish sultan has promised to accept Jews and treat them well. We want to leave for Constantinople as soon as we can."

"The Muslims don't mind that we practice our faith," Grandfather adds. "They won't force us to convert."

Tía Mazal sees the disappointment in Mother's face. "Do not worry, hermanica. You will have plenty of time to rest and recover your strength. We are not leaving for a while!"

Mother's hands tremble, and she struggles to speak. "Querida familia, I don't know if I can survive another journey by sea. It was the sea that made me a widow . . ."

Grandmother rises and helps Mother to her feet. "We will worry about that when the time comes—not for many, many months. Now come, hijica, it is time to sleep. Let me take you to your bed, the way I used to do when you were a little girl. I placed rose blossoms on your pillow so you can enjoy the scent."

Tía Mazal leads me to the bed that I will share with her, and Tío Yehuda leads Isaac and Jacob to theirs.

I remember how Father sang to me when we were on the journey. *Durme, durme,* I hear him whispering, and I sleep without fear, only with sorrow.

15

Poems That She Wore Like Jewels

Early every morning, Grandfather, Tío Yehuda, and Isaac and Jacob don their prayer shawls and pray in memory of Father. They chant from the Torah that miraculously survived the journey from Toledo without a scratch or tear.

Girls aren't taught the prayers, or to chant from the Torah. I listen from the kitchen as I help Grandmother and Tía Mazal with the cooking and memorize what I can.

But Tío Yehuda doesn't mind telling me about the printing press whenever I'm curious. Right now he is preparing to print a special Haggadah for Passover, telling the story of when the Jews left Egypt for freedom in a new land.

"It is not the first time we have had to seek our freedom," Tío Yehuda remarks. "That is why the Haggadah will be printed in two languages—Hebrew and Spanish—with commentaries by the rabbis. Even though the king and queen expelled us, they cannot take our language from us."

Isaac and Jacob are constantly at Tío Yehuda's side, learning every detail of how the printing press works and becoming perfect apprentices to our uncle and grandfather.

Isaac reviews the texts with care, letter by letter, while Jacob is fast and agile with his hands and binds the books with strength and ease.

Tío Yehuda is pleased and praises Isaac and Jacob. He says that next year when we move to Constantinople, he will expand his printing press and they will all work together and hire several new apprentices.

I too offered to help with the family business. I demonstrated to my uncle how I could read both Hebrew and Spanish so swiftly I didn't need to take a breath between words.

"My oh my, you are talented, Benvenida!" he said. And although he looked at me proudly, he added, "But this is not an occupation for girls."

So now instead I work side by side with Tía Mazal most mornings. She is teaching me how to sew, and we are making pretty nightgowns and robes that she will sell to the families of new brides for their trousseaux. "You are learning well," she says to me. "Maybe you will be a bride before too long. When we arrive in Constantinople, we will take our time finding you a good husband."

"And why are you not married?" I dare ask.

"I have been a widow since I was young and never married again."

"And what about Tío Yehuda?"

"Your uncle also became a widower when he was young. That is why we are like two children living in the house with our mother and father."

Tía Mazal sighs, and she recites,

> *I look for you early,*
> *my rock and my refuge,*
> > *offering you worship*
> > *morning and night ...*

"That's from a poem by Shlomo Ibn Gabirol. He lived centuries ago in Málaga and then in Saragossa and Granada. My husband used to recite his poems to me, but I only remember a few verses here and there."

"That's beautiful," I say. "I wrote poems when we lived in Toledo. That's why the hem of my dress was all bunched up when we arrived. I hid the poems in the seams."

Tía Mazal is astounded. "Wait, you mean you don't just read, but you can write too?"

"Yes, Tía. Writing makes me feel better. And, you know, my favorite poet is Qasmuna—she was a Jewish woman too, though she wrote in Arabic."

Tía Mazal shakes her head. "Benvenida, I'm afraid writing poetry is not an occupation for girls. It is good you can read. Your future husband will be glad to have an educated wife, but go no further, my sweet girl."

I am disappointed and go back to my sewing without saying another word on the subject.

But the next day, Tía Mazal surprises me when I take my seat beside her to sew. She smiles and edges closer to me. "I've been thinking about what I said to you yesterday, hijica. How you said writing makes you feel better. I believe that is a good thing, so I grabbed some parchment and ink. Continue to write your poems, dear Benvenida."

"Thank you, Tía Mazal!"

In between sewing, Tía Mazal urges me to write. I scribble poems about the girl I used to be, the girl who knew where home was, the girl who thought she'd walk along Toledo's cobblestoned streets and gaze at its golden hills forever and ever.

> *Once there was a girl who wrote poems,*
> *poems that she wore like jewels,*
> *poems as beautiful as the nightingales*
> *that sang for her in the courtyard . . .*

Tía Mazal enjoys listening to my poems. Now she even tells me I must never give up writing.

One day she surprises me again when she presents me with a new dress. "Here, try this on. Let's see how it fits," she says.

The dress is so soft and easy to move around in, I feel as if I have wings.

"Tía Mazal, I love it!"

"It's a special dress. Do you see what I've done, Benvenida? Look at the folds of fabric, the deep pockets I've created in the seams of the dress. There's space to hide your poems, and no one will notice. Wherever you go, your poems can travel with you."

That evening I store some poems in the dress, and I wonder about the parchment I hid in the stone wall of our old house. Is it still there? And if it is, perhaps someday someone will find it?

16

A Reunion Amid Eggplants

One of my favorite things to do in Naples is to go to the market with Mother and Tía Mazal. Today we are hoping to buy eggplants because I've been missing Father and feeling nostalgic for the eggplant-and-honey dish we enjoyed in Toledo. Grandmother says she has a jar of honey, and if we find the eggplants, she will happily make the dish for us. As we wander through the market, we finally come across a farmer selling beautiful purple eggplants. That's when I see a familiar-looking woman with a baby. Could it be?

"Mother, Tía Mazal, wait here for me! I think I see Naomi!"

I run after the woman and shout, "Naomi, is that you?"

The woman swings her head around, and when she sees me, her face lights up. "Benvenida, yes! Is that really you?"

"Yes, it's me!" I say. "And look how big Preciada has grown!"

"Yes, my precious baby. Born on the journey out of Spain."

We hug each other and then go to where Mother and Tía Mazal are waiting.

"Mother, it really is Naomi, with baby Preciada!"

Like me, Mother can't believe her eyes. "Oh my, oh my, how wonderful that you are here! And how the baby has grown!"

"My sweet Preciada is eight months old," Naomi says. "And already starting to crawl!"

"I am so glad to see her," Mother says. Then she becomes sad. "I never thought I'd see anyone from our group again. We lost so many along the way. I lost my beloved husband at sea."

"Oh no, I am so sorry. May his memory be a blessing," Naomi says. She hugs Mother and then kisses her baby's soft fuzzy head. "So much loss, but we have been fortunate. We were taken in by my great-aunt here in Naples."

"Will you come visit with us for a little while?" Tía Mazal asks. "We live nearby."

"I would love to," Naomi says. "And that means we must be neighbors."

"May I carry Preciada?" I ask.

"Of course, Benvenida, here you go. Be warned—she is heavier than she looks!"

Preciada wraps her chubby arms around my neck as I perch her on my hip. She does grow heavy as we climb the hill to our house, but I don't mind if my arms get sore. Preciada is such a sweet baby. She keeps turning to look at her mother and then back at me and finally smiles as if she remembers me perfectly.

Once at the house, we set a blanket down on the floor and let Preciada crawl from end to end. When Preciada grows tired of playing, Naomi nurses her, then passes her to me. I sing the lullaby I sang to her before she was born, the one Father sang to me. *Durme, durme, sin ansia y dolor...* And in a few moments, she falls asleep in my arms.

Afterward, Naomi comes to visit with Preciada every day. To entertain her, I play my tambourine, and she claps her little hands. I try to remember every Spanish song I know, and I sing them to her. She especially loves the one about the girl in the sea tower, and for that she claps the loudest.

17

I Will Lift My Voice and Be Heard

Our last few months in Naples pass quickly. But everyone worries as we hear stories of cruelties inflicted upon Jews trying to find homes in new lands.

In Portugal children were snatched by Christian families and forced to convert.

A group of Jews who tried to sail south from the port of Cádiz to the kingdom of Fez died in a terrible fire.

"Things will get worse here too," Tío Yehuda says. "We must not wait much longer. We need to go where we can be safe and flourish for many years, for generation upon generation."

When Tía Mazal tells Naomi our plans, she says, "And you and baby Preciada and your husband must come with us."

"We will, we will," Naomi whispers. "If we can . . ."

"Do not worry about the cost," Grandfather says. "You are now like our family."

"Gracias, gracias," Naomi responds with tears in her eyes. "I am so grateful."

Mother cries, "Traveling on those choppy sea waters again, I will surely die. My beloved Samuelico will call to me! He will want me to join him!"

Grandfather tries to reassure her. "Hijica, I promise you that you will not suffer on this voyage. We have heard of others who have gone to Constantinople, and they have not been mistreated. They will receive us warmly when we arrive. The sultan has issued a royal decree stating that Jews can settle wherever they wish and must be welcomed."

"I have received word from friends there who will help us establish our new printing press," Tío Yehuda announces. "Isaac and Jacob have learned so much. Our families will work together and joyfully share bread again at the table as we once did in Toledo."

As the day of our voyage approaches, I take Mother's hand. "Don't be afraid, Mother. Father wants you to live, and he wants Isaac and Jacob to live, and he wants me to live. We will honor him by seeking freedom."

Mother's eyes fill with tears. "Benvenida, may it be so. From your lips to the ears of nuestro Dio!"

I give her Amina's handkerchief and tell her, "Mother, let's go forth with faith in El Dio. In the new land we'll hear the nightingales sing again. And though I can't be a hazan like Father because I am a girl, I will lift my voice and be heard."

Just as Grandfather promises, the voyage to Constantinople goes smoothly. The ship is not overcrowded, and we don't suffer from the seasickness and fear we experienced on the way to Naples.

When the ship docks, I look out at the vast city that embraces the Sea of Marmara and inhale the salty air. From now on, this is the air I'll breathe. Constantinople is even grander than Naples and is totally breathtaking with its gold domes shimmering in the sun.

Can it be that at last we've arrived at a place where all kinds of people—Muslims, Christians, Jews—are allowed to live together side by side? And live peacefully?

I repeat to myself the name of this city where I will now live, Constantinople. I'm wearing my new dress, and I pat the poems that I stored in its seams. *What new ones will I write here?* I wonder.

When we step down to set foot on dry land, I see an old man sitting by the edge of the sea, singing. He plays a pear-shaped instrument that resembles a lute. The sound from its strings, sweet and haunting and melodic, touches my soul.

"What is he playing?" I ask.

Grandfather says, "It's called an oud."

"It's so lovely! I want to play the oud."

"Then you shall," he replies with a smile. "But first, let's find our new home."

I am blessed to have a grandfather who is so good to me.

I promise myself that wherever my new home shall be, I'll sing the old songs that came with me across the sea, and I'll sing them playing the oud.

Perhaps someday Tía Mazal will get her wish, and I will be a bride and then a mother. Or maybe I won't marry, and I'll teach baby Preciada all that I know. One way or another, I will pass along the songs that have given me such comfort to the next generation, so they won't be lost.

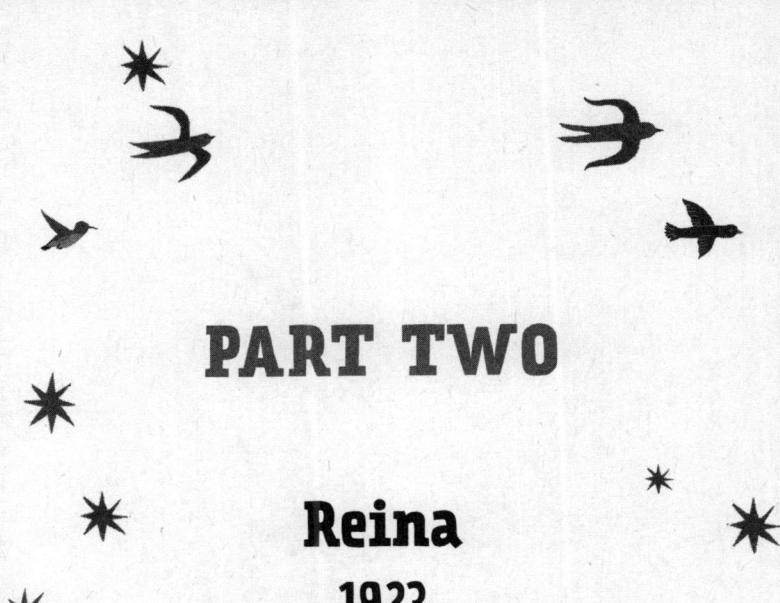

PART TWO

Reina
1923

18

I Came Into the World Carrying a Bundle of Sadness

I sit on my bed, strumming a tune on my mother's oud, trying to remember the words to a song she played for me. It's a sad song about three sisters.

Mima says I love sad songs because I have a melancholy soul. *Hüzün* is the Turkish word she uses to describe my temperament. In Spanish, it is *triste*. Mima says I came into the world carrying a bundle of sadness. Even as a baby, it wasn't easy to make me smile or laugh.

But now it's time to put away the oud and get ready for the parade. My younger sisters come running into the room, calling for me.

"Hurry, Reina!"

"Come on, Reina!"

Suzi, who is ten, and Dina, who is eight, are decked out in their finest dresses and have satin bows in their hair. We share the same dark eyes and dark wavy hair, just like Mima.

Suzi looks at me in my everyday dress and shakes her head. "Reina, get ready!"

Dina adds, "Mima and Papa are waiting. We don't want to miss the parade!"

"Don't worry, hermanicas. I'll be fast."

I quickly put on my best dress and comb my hair into a bun. As the eldest and already twelve, I feel too old to wear a ribbon in my hair.

We lock arms and stride into the main room, where Mima and Papa are finishing their coffee.

Papa puts down his cup and says, "Time for the parade, eh? We must all celebrate our nation's independence. No more sultans for us. We will see if this President Atatürk can make us into a modern nation." Then he chuckles. "I'll have to trade my fez for a European-style felt hat."

Mima sighs. "I hope that is all you'll have to do to be part of this new nation."

Never one to hold my tongue, I chime in. "They say our new president will give girls as good an education as boys. Let us even become pilots if we wish! And he doesn't think women should have to hide themselves in robes and veils when they go out."

"Shush," Papa says firmly. "Reina, you're reading too many newspapers!"

"I'm sorry, Papa."

I know it's best to just apologize quickly, as Papa often has a bad temper.

But he smiles and says, "It's all right. Just remember your place, hijica."

Mima continues to voice her worries. "I hope we won't be forced to speak only Turkish. We speak so many beautiful languages in this land."

"No one can take our language from us," Papa replies. "If we've managed to continue speaking our Spanish for hundreds of years, without ever returning to Spain, then we will go on speaking it forever."

I'm relieved to hear Papa say this. I too love our Spanish, and our Jewish community continues to speak it even though we were forced out of Spain centuries ago.

We are about to leave when we hear the boys next door, Sadik, Emir, and Nazim, coming out into our shared courtyard. They are the same ages as the three of us, and my sisters and I grew up playing with them. They celebrate Ramadan, the Muslim month of fasting, and at the end of it they used to invite us to break the fast, and then we used to invite them to break the fast with us after Yom Kippur. I have good memories of laughing and stuffing our faces with too many sweet dates.

Lately, though, Papa calls us inside whenever the boys are out. He tells Mima to give us more indoor chores after school. So now we're always helping our mother with the cooking and cleaning and even her lace making. Papa's a goldsmith, and his work has suffered from his worsening eyesight and shaking hands. Mima earns most of our money selling her lace to a wealthy storeowner from Istanbul who visits every month to buy it at a good price.

"Close the door," Papa tells me. "We will wait till the boys leave. You and your sisters spend too much time with them."

"But, Papa, they're our neighbors, and we barely see them at all anymore."

"As it should be," Papa says. "Reina, listen to me. You are twelve now, and it's not proper to play with boys. They are good boys, but they are boys. And they are Muslim. Since you are the eldest, I put my trust in you to set a good example for Suzi and Dina. So no more mingling, you understand?"

"Yes, Papa." I say this even though I don't agree. I want to please Papa in the moment, as it feels nice when he shows his love for me.

"Good, that's settled, then." Papa reaches into the pocket of his woolen suit jacket, where he stashes sesame sweets and hard candies, and pulls out some for all of us. With a laugh, he says, "Is everyone ready to go to the parade? We're a modern independent nation now. Haven't you heard? We must celebrate!"

19

The Parade

Mima holds on to Papa's elbow, and he leads the way down the cobblestoned streets.

It's a Monday, but schools and stores are closed for the celebration, so everyone in the neighborhood is heading to the parade—Greek, Armenian, and Muslim families, along with a few Spanish Jewish families like ours. We all greet one another politely.

"What a warm and sunny day for the end of October!"

"Surely a good sign for our country!"

Looking out at the blue waves of the Marmara, we approach the port, and I feel calmer than I have in a long time. At last, the wars that have been raging since I was born are over.

Too many men from our community were killed in the Turkish War of Independence—husbands, fathers, uncles, brothers, sons, cousins. I thank God that Papa was too old to be conscripted into the army. When Mima and Papa were younger, it must not have mattered that he was twenty years older than her. Now strangers see them together and they think he's her father, and that embarrasses them, though they smile and try to make light of it. As Mima says to Papa, "Be grateful. It's thanks to your age that you're still with us."

We find a corner where we can be together amid the crowd. That's when we spot my aunt, Tía Zimbul, leaning against her housekeeper, Diamanta, who doubles as a helper. Tía Zimbul has barely stepped outside in the past two years. When my dear cousin Rafi died, she took to her bed for the longest time. She suffered terribly because her only child had been killed on the battlefield and his body wouldn't be sent home. To bury him in the cemetery and at least be able to visit his grave would have been a comfort, but she'd been denied that too.

"Buen día, Tía Zimbul," we say now, taking turns hugging her lightly, as if she might break.

"Buen día, my dear family," she responds. "It was Diamanta who insisted I come to the parade. So here I am. Let's see how long I can stay on my feet."

"You can also lean on me, Tía Zimbul, if you'd like," I say.

"Thank you, Reina, I will do that." And I feel her relax against my side.

"Look how many people have come! All of us are hopeful for a better future," I tell her.

"Yes, the future Rafi gave his life for," she says. "My dear sweet Rafi."

Just at that moment the parade begins, and everyone cheers. We watch as the soldiers march by, carrying the flag of our new nation of Turkey, bright red with the crescent and the star.

"We are all Turkish now!" someone in the crowd yells to more cheering, and I see the worry on the faces of Papa and Mima, who fear what changes might be coming and what it means for us.

After the parade ends, the street peddlers appear, selling honey-and-fig and rosewater-and-pistachio flavors of ice cream, so refreshing in the unusually warm weather. Everyone rushes to get ice cream and forgets they had any worries.

We say goodbye to Tía Zimbul and watch her walk away on unsteady feet with Diamanta. As we climb the hill back to our home, we run into our neighbors Ahmet and Afrah and their boys, Sadik, Emir, and Nazim, and Papa can't make us avoid them now.

"Buen día," Ahmet says to Papa in our Spanish.

"Merhaba," Papa replies in Arabic.

Mima and Afrah nod to one another politely and walk the rest of the way together, behind the men.

We children follow, and there's a moment when I stop to look down at the sea from the top of the hill, and Sadik, who is also twelve, stops too.

"The fireworks will be going on all night in Istanbul. We'll be able to catch a glimpse of them here in Silivri. There's going to be a party at the port for us young people. You should come. I never get to see you anymore, and I'm sure it will be beautiful."

"You go. I'd like to, but my father would never let me go to a party," I tell him, and I rush ahead and catch up with Suzi and Dina.

Our two families cross through our shared courtyard, and we all say goodbye and wish one another a good lunch.

Once inside, I light the stove while my sisters set the table.

I warm up the spinach bulemas and the potato-and-cheese borekas that we made the day before, following recipes that go back generations. I empty a jar of olives into a bowl. I cut up chunks of watermelon, sweet karpuz, removing the seeds and mixing it with pungent kashkaval cheese.

We sit down to lunch, and Suzi mentions hearing about the fireworks tonight.

"Can we go? Can we go?" my little sister Dina begs.

Papa finishes savoring a boreka and wipes his lips with a napkin. "These borekas are more delicious every day. How lucky I am to have a wife and three daughters who cook so well for me."

Then he smiles at Suzi and Dina. "Hijicas, we are all staying home tonight. I think we have celebrated enough."

20

I Believe I Should Be Free

After lunch, Mima and Papa prepare for their nap.

"You must stay inside, out of the heat, and rest too," Papa says. "And, Reina, remember what I said. You be an example to your sisters."

He gives me a stern look and waits for my reply.

"I understand, Papa," I say.

After our parents go to their room, Suzi and Dina and I finish cleaning and putting the dishes away.

It's muggy inside with all the windows and curtains closed to keep out the sun, and I start to feel faint. "Let's go out to the courtyard for a bit," I say. "To get a little air."

"But Papa told us to stay inside," Suzi said.

And Dina, copying Suzi, says, "We have to listen to Papa."

"I need some air," I tell them. "And you know they'll sleep for hours, so they won't even know we stepped out."

Suzi and Dina don't budge.

"I'm going. Stay if you like."

And then they follow me, as they always do.

Once outside we find Sadik, Emir, and Nazim sitting in the shade on their side of the courtyard.

"Are your parents napping too?" I ask Sadik.

He nods, his brown eyes glowing in the light of the afternoon sun.

Emir, ten like Suzi, and Nazim, eight like Dina, start chasing each other around the courtyard. They're still children. But Sadik and I, being twelve, feel too grown-up to play tag.

Sadik points to one of the chairs, and I join him.

"We don't see you and your sisters very much anymore. Is everything all right?" he asks. "It's not because of illness, God forbid, or anything else bad, is it?"

"We're fine. Do not worry."

"Mashallah," he says, smiling.

I smile back, hesitating to say more. But it's hard to keep secrets from Sadik. We took our first steps together in this courtyard and learned to run by chasing each other.

"The truth is my father doesn't want us to leave the house because we're girls and getting older. Mostly, it's because I'm twelve now, and if I act dishonorably, I will bring shame to the family."

This upsets Sadik, and he says, "But how can your father not trust you to be good? And how can your father not trust me and my brothers to be good? We have always been good."

"I know, I know," I tell Sadik. "But my father is old-fashioned. He's already starting to worry about our prospects for marriage! But hopefully things are changing. Look at how our new president wants girls to get good educations too. Wants them to be free to become anything they want!"

Sadik shakes his head. "Reina, I agree education is important for girls too. But I don't think our president understands how religious people think. You know my mother wears a headscarf because she is Muslim—but she likes wearing it when she's out. I don't want her to feel ashamed to wear it just because he thinks we are too modern for that."

I nod, not sure what to say. I've always seen his mother, Afrah, wearing pretty headscarves and can't imagine her any other way. But I never thought about whether she enjoyed wearing them or if she had to because of her religion, the way, in my religion, females can't touch the Torah scrolls or sit near men at the temple. And some very religious Jewish women also cover their heads with a scarf.

"I agree, Sadik," I finally reply. "Your mother should wear her headscarf if she wants to, and she shouldn't feel bad about it. That's what freedom really is about—having a choice."

Suzi and Dina come skipping over, followed by Emir and Nazim. The four of them are giggling and covered in sweat from chasing one another. The bows in Suzi's and Dina's hair have come undone.

"Aren't you and Sadik going to play tag with us?" Suzi asks.

Dina adds, "You two look like old people, just sitting and talking!"

I look up at the sky, now a pale shade of blue. We need to go inside, before Mima and Papa wake up.

"There's no more time to play," I say. "Here, let me fix the bows in your hair."

"Just a little longer, please," Suzi begs.

Dina then begs, "Please, please!"

Emir and Nazim stand waiting, in hopes of playing more.

"Sorry, we'll get in trouble. We have to go," I insist.

I retie the bows in my sisters' hair and tell them to straighten their dresses.

As Suzi and Dina walk toward our house, Sadik whispers to me. "Reina, please come tonight. The sky will be lit up, and it will be different from any other night. It'll be historic! Tell your father you shouldn't miss it and I will watch over you."

"It's impossible. And anyway, Sadik, I don't need anyone watching over me!"

"You're right. You should be able to do what you want, Reina. Try to come outside if you can. I'll be here waiting for you."

I shrug before walking away. Sadik's comment about watching over me has really irked me.

Like our new president, I believe I should be free.

21

In the Sea There Is a Tower

I wait until Suzi and Dina are sound asleep to slip out of the bed the three of us share. I hear Mima and Papa snoring. It is as safe a moment to go as it will ever be.

My heart pounds. I've never done anything so willful. But I take a deep breath, change into a clean dress, slip on my shoes, and throw the blue sweater that Mima knit for me over my shoulders. And I reach for the oud.

Mima and Papa keep an extra key to the house in a bowl in the kitchen. I grab it and go out the door, quiet as a thief.

Outside the air is still warm. I look around and don't see Sadik. I wonder if he's let me down, but a part of me is relieved.

"Reina, here I am," he whispers.

He's changed into a shirt with long sleeves and a gray vest. He looks very grown-up.

"You brought your oud," he says. "I've missed hearing you play it in the courtyard. Now I have to listen through the walls."

"I didn't realize you could hear me. Is it too loud?"

"Not at all. It's beautiful. I don't understand the Spanish songs you sing, but I like them very much."

"Thank you. My mother taught them to me. I thought I'd play a song tonight, it being historic and all." I smile at Sadik, and he smiles back.

"Yes! That will be nice. Let's go before it gets late."

We take the same route downhill from the high side of town as we took earlier with our families to go to the parade. I've never been out in the street at night without Mima and Papa and my sisters. Walking side by side with Sadik isn't any different, I tell myself. We've known each other forever, and he's like a brother.

As we cross through the last alleyways and approach the port, we hear the distant blasts of fireworks coming from Istanbul. The sky turns bright with streaks of pink and purple. It's so lit up that for a moment it doesn't look like it's nighttime. I dare to let myself feel happy that I get to witness this.

"Hello, Reina" and "Hello, Sadik," everyone calls out as we approach.

I look around and see many familiar faces from the neighborhood. I recognize the Armenian and Greek kids who go to church with their families, the Muslim Turkish kids who go to the mosque with their families. And I recognize one of the Jewish boys from our synagogue—Benny, whose father works as a water carrier, delivering water to the houses from the town fountain, la fuentezica, as we call it.

I am so entranced by the fireworks that it takes me a moment to realize I'm the only girl here. When I do, my stomach sinks, but I remind myself that I'm not afraid of the boys. I know so many of the ones here and trust them. But that doesn't mean the news won't spread that I was the only girl, and then Papa could find out.

Sadik quickly sizes up the situation too. "Reina, let's go home."

We turn to leave, and Benny calls out, "Reina, play us a song on the oud."

"Another day," I tell him.

"Just one song, Reina," Benny insists.

Maybe it's the excitement of the fireworks lighting up the sky, or the realization that no matter what I do I'm going to get punished, or maybe it's that on this day I feel I have as much right to be there as the boys, but I agree to play one of my favorite songs that Mima's taught me.

> *En la mar hay una torre,*
> *en la torre una ventana,*
> *en la ventana una hija*
> *que a los marineros llama.*
>
> *In the sea there is a tower,*
> *in the tower there is a window,*
> *at the window a daughter*
> *who calls to the sailors.*

"Beautiful!" Benny yells, and they all clap for me. Then he says, "But that sounds like a song of forbidden love, Reina. That must mean there's someone here you secretly love."

I feel the heat rising to my cheeks. "No, no, no. I'm too young to know anything about love. It's just an old song from Spain."

Teasing me, he asks again, "Are you sure there isn't anyone here you love?"

He reaches for my oud. I'm afraid he'll break it, so I try to pull it away. He grasps the oud's neck and scratches it with his fingernails before he lets me have it again.

"Stop!" Sadik yells. "Leave Reina alone!"

"Who are you to tell me what to do?" Benny yells back.

The other boys begin to assemble into two groups, one on Benny's side and the other on Sadik's side, and I'm afraid there will be a fight.

Sadik whispers, "Come on, Reina. Let's go!"

We run as fast as we can through the alleyways, the cobblestones rubbing against the soles of my shoes. We're panting as we climb to the top of the hill, above the Marmara. Then we take a deep breath and enter the courtyard in silence, barely breathing.

"Good night, Reina. Let's pray no one will say a word about tonight."

"Everything will be fine," I reply, more confident than I feel.

In the dark I see him smiling. "I'm glad I got to hear you

sing and play the oud without a wall between us. You sing like a nightingale."

"Thank you, Sadik. Good night."

I slip inside and place the key in the bowl. I hear the snores of Mima and Papa, and I slide into place between Suzi and Dina, who are sound asleep. I wasn't gone very long. Maybe my adventure will go unnoticed.

I fall asleep, remembering the night sky streaked with the gorgeous light from the fireworks, and how the sea waves seemed to accompany me as I sang and played Mima's oud.

22

I'll Keep Listening to You Through the Walls

I get ready for school as usual the next morning, with my sisters. We put on our uniforms and sit down to our breakfast of tea and sesame-topped bizkochikos, our favorite biscuits, while Mima tidies the kitchen and Papa reads the newspaper with a pair of thick glasses.

I finish the last bite of my bizkochiko and leap to my feet. I can't bear to be in the house, hiding my lie from Mima and Papa.

"Are you ready?" I say to Suzi and Dina. "Let's go."

"But it's not time yet," Suzi says, looking at the clock Mima keeps in the kitchen.

Dina adds, "What's the rush?"

"If we leave now, we can walk more slowly. Wouldn't that be nice?"

"Yes, why don't you all go along to school now?" Mima agrees.

I go outside first, and there in the courtyard is Sadik, sitting on one of the chairs where we sat talking the day before. His face is streaked with tears, his hair tousled, and he has on the same clothes he wore last night. He nods at me but doesn't speak.

"What happened, Sadik?" I ask before my sisters join me.

"Nothing. I will tell you later."

"Don't you have to go to school?"

"I'll be late today."

He slips away before Suzi and Dina see him.

It's a long day at our Jewish school for girls. I am so worried I feel sick to my stomach.

I keep telling myself I did nothing wrong. I went to enjoy the fireworks from Istanbul and to celebrate our national independence and sang a song and played the oud. That's all. Papa said no, but he always does, and I am a girl who wants to be free.

Somehow, I make it through the day. Arriving home with my sisters, I see that Mima has hung the laundry to dry in the courtyard, where it sways in the breeze.

"It smells so clean," I say to Mima.

Mima sighs. "Everything is bright white again," she says. "But what a lot of work to boil the clothes in the large pots with the bluing powder."

"I'm sorry I couldn't help you, Mima."

"You concentrate on your books, hijica."

"I'll help you bring in the clothes from the courtyard. Afterward, Mima, can you teach me another Spanish song?"

"Not today, I'm too tired."

I pour water into a basin and take it to the bedroom to

rinse my face. Then I change out of my uniform and put on a loose dress.

Suzi and Dina are playing with their dolls, as they like to do after school, and have forgotten all about me.

I return to help Mima with the laundry. As I'm about to step out into the courtyard, Mima asks, "Did you scratch the oud? Didn't I tell you to be careful with it?"

"I am careful with the oud. Very careful. I must have accidentally scratched it."

"How?"

"With my fingernails."

Mima takes hold of my hands and holds them up in the air. "Look at your hands, Reina. How is that possible? You don't have long nails."

"It must have just happened, Mima. I am so sorry!"

She turns away, and I slip out into the courtyard hesitantly, not sure if Sadik will be there and if he'll tell me why he was so disheveled in the morning.

I unclip the laundry from the clothesline and pile everything in the basket. As I'm finishing, Sadik comes out. He has washed up and changed his clothes, but now I notice the bruise on his cheek.

"Are you going to tell me what happened?" I ask.

"Last night, I went back to the port after we said goodbye, and got into a fight with Benny."

"What? Why did you do that?"

"I was angry at how Benny treated you . . ."

"Sadik, now I'm definitely going to get in trouble!"

"No you won't. No one will believe Benny or his friends. You just say they're lying if anyone says anything about where you were last night."

"My mother already noticed the scratch on the oud."

"Oh no."

"I better go inside." I pick up the basket and turn to leave.

"Reina?"

"What, Sadik?"

"I'm sorry I insisted that you go to the party with me. I thought there would be other girls. I don't understand why the girls weren't there. We've all known each other in the neighborhood since we were little. We've always gotten along with each other, no matter if we're Muslim or Jewish or Christian. We're all good kids. Aren't we?"

He has such an earnest look on his face.

"We are good, Sadik."

"Please don't be angry, Reina."

"I'm not. But I can't stay here talking. My mother will wonder about me. And I probably shouldn't come outside to the courtyard anymore."

Sadik smiles sadly. "If I don't see you, I'll keep listening to you through the walls. Please keep singing those beautiful old songs and playing the oud."

23

To Me, You Are Dead

I bring in the clean laundry and find the house filled with the aromas of Papa's favorite foods, which Mima is preparing for dinner—the agristada soup with just the right mix of lemon and egg, the dolmas made from tomatoes filled with rice and meat and a bit of parsley, and the sweet eggplant dish, the berenjenas con miel that he especially adores. Mima has also made baklava for dessert, and it's soaking up the sugary syrup she has poured over the flaky layers of pastry and walnuts.

Papa sits at the head of the table as always. Mima serves him first and gives him the largest portions. Then she serves each of us in turn and finally serves herself.

"Everything is delicious, cooked to perfection," Papa says.

Mima smiles. "I'm glad you enjoy it."

Then I help Mima clear the table and serve the plates of sweet baklava. All is peaceful until Papa eats his last bite. Then he wipes his mouth with his napkin and suddenly his expression changes. He looks at me with disgust, and I know I am in trouble.

He sends my sisters to our room and turns to me coldly. "I heard you were in the street last night, Reina. That you were with Sadik. That you had the nerve to bring your mother's oud to the seaport and sing songs for the neighborhood boys. Didn't I forbid you from going out? How did you dare to disobey me? You have shamed yourself, Reina. And you have shamed your family."

I wait for him to slap me. But what comes feels worse than that.

My father looks at me as if I am nothing and says, "You are not my daughter anymore. To me, you are dead."

I can't believe I am hearing such harsh words from my own father!

"Papa! I did nothing wrong!" I start to explain, but he will not listen. He just stands up and walks to his and Mima's bedroom and shuts the door.

He says I am no longer his daughter, which means I no longer have a father.

I think about how Mima says that I came into the world carrying a bundle of sadness. Now I have more than a bundle to carry—I have a boulder.

I will carry the weight of his proclamation with me always.

But I am determined to stay alive. I will not let that boulder crush me.

24

Once You Are There, Don't Look Back, Hijica

I'm not allowed to go to school anymore.

I'm not allowed to go outside.

I'm not allowed to have dinner with my family at the table. I have to eat by myself, standing up in the kitchen after everyone has been served, and all I get are the scraps.

I'm not allowed to sleep in the bed with Suzi and Dina. I have to sleep on the floor.

I'm not allowed to go to our temple, our Kal, on Shabbat and be with other Jews.

At least Mima and Suzi and Dina still speak to me when Papa isn't around, but Papa continues to act like I don't exist.

Days and weeks pass without Papa saying a word to me. So it is Mima who relays the news that Papa is sending me away to Cuba with Tía Zimbul.

Tía Zimbul has decided she can't bear to remain in Silivri. Everything reminds her of Rafi, my dear cousin who died in the war. Now I am to be her companion, as well as servant, in Cuba. I will do her cooking and cleaning, iron her clothes, and wipe the tears from her eyes.

But the news gets more shocking.

Papa has agreed to marry me off to a distant cousin who fled to Cuba years ago so he could escape fighting in the War of Independence. His name is Moshico, and he has agreed to wait three years, until I am fifteen, and then he will marry me.

Mima tells me this part of the news with tears in her eyes.

"I know it seems terrible, Reina, but perhaps it is for the best," Mima says. "No one will marry you in Silivri."

"But I'm only twelve, Mima! Everybody will forget in a few years. And the world is changing!"

"Not fast enough. Your reputation is tarnished here, and no one forgets anything. This could also harm the reputation of your sisters, so it's best if you go to Cuba. I'm sorry, Reina."

I have so many questions as I reel from what Mima's telling me. Mostly, though, I'm scared.

The next day I ask Mima about one of the things worrying me most. "Tell me what to do when I meet Moshico."

"Do not worry, hijica. You just smile at him and thank him for taking you as his wife. You do not have to do anything more. He will wait three years, until you are fifteen, and then he will marry you, and by then you will be older and you will know what to do."

"And if I don't like him, Mima?"

"Why won't you like him, mi Reina? He has been kind enough to take you as his wife after the mistake you made. You must treat him with respect and gratitude and do everything to make him happy."

"But how will I know how to make him happy?"

"He will teach you. And you will learn. That is how it was with me and your papa. I am grateful he was chosen for me. He has been a good husband."

She smiles; then she turns, and I see her brush away a tear. Now I understand why Papa is so much older than Mima.

I have so many more questions, but Mima doesn't want to talk. "Enough, enough. Your sisters will be home any minute and then your papa. Count yourself lucky that you are going away to Cuba. You can start a new life there. And you will be good company to Tía Zimbul. She has suffered so much with the loss of her son. She will start a new life in Cuba too. Both of you together. Once you are there, don't look back, hijica."

"But I will want to come back and see you again, Mima. And my dear sisters."

"And your papa?"

I take a breath. I know that if I don't say Papa too, it will be like casting the evil eye on him, wishing for something bad to happen to him.

"Yes, and Papa."

Mima looks sad and weary again. "He has done what he needed to do. It has been very difficult for him. You are too young to understand, but he weeps for you as he has wept for the ancestors who fled Spain during the expulsion."

I try to imagine Papa crying for me. Does he truly feel bad he's sending me away? It is so strange to be told you are dead when you are still alive. I keep hoping he'll give me a nod or a glance, but he offers me no kindness, no love, no forgiveness. And so the anger and sadness continue to grow inside me like weeds, leaving no room for my heart to feel joy. I pray the sunshine in Cuba will allow a little flower to grow in me.

25

Song of the Sisters

All I can do as I wait for the day to arrive when I will leave for Cuba is help Mima with chores while Suzi and Dina are in school and Papa is out peddling the few things he still has left to sell from the time he was a goldsmith.

Mima tries to teach me everything I'll need to know about managing a house. I can tell she feels pity for me and blames herself for not having been a better mother and stopped me from being so rebellious. But I know it is not her fault.

And then one day she asks, "Who scratched the oud?" and I tell her everything that happened the night of the fireworks—about Benny and that it was his fingernails that left that ugly scratch on the neck of the oud.

"But Benny did not touch you? And Sadik did not touch you?"

"No, Mima, no one touched me. I only sang one song and played the oud."

"You were wrong to do even that. People talk. And a girl needs to be pure. Do you understand?"

"I know, Mima, I know. I am sorry. I just wanted to be free for a change. And there were supposed to be other girls at the party, not that it would have mattered..."

We both begin to cry, and Mima takes me in her arms and says, "Reina, my eldest daughter, you are so precious and such a help to me. I don't know what I will do without you. But I take consolation in knowing you can take care of yourself. I just wish I could do more..."

"I will be all right, Mima. And there is something you can do. Please teach me more songs before I go. Playing music is the only thing that makes me feel good anymore."

"Yes, I promise I will teach you what more I know of the old Spanish songs. Just a few minutes a day, when we are alone, all right?"

"Thank you, Mima. I will remember those songs as if they are etched in my soul."

After that, for most of my remaining days we sit together and sing.

Mima teaches me all the verses to my favorite song, the one about the three sisters.

> *Tres ermanikas eran,*
> *tres ermanikas son.*
> *Las dos están kazadas,*
> *la chika en perdision.*
> *Su padre de vergüenza*
> *kastiyo le fregó...*

*sin puerta i sin vintana
ke no entre varón.*

*There once were three sisters,
three sisters they are.
Two are married,
the youngest has been ruined.
Her father, ashamed,
built her a tower...
without doors or windows
so no man can enter.*

Mima and I take turns playing the song on the oud, passing it back and forth to each other, and we cry for the sister who has been ruined and banished to a tower by her father, that sister who is me.

26

Sadik's Goodbye

Mima trusts me enough that, now and then, when we're alone, she'll go visit one of her cousins who lives nearby to have tea and bizkochikos and forget about her worries.

I imagine how tiring it must be for her to be my prison guard, as Papa demands she be. She needs air and light and the sea breeze and sunshine. I need those things too, but I am resigned to not having them while I wait to leave for Cuba.

It's like the whole world has forgotten me, and I'm already gone.

Soon I will be crossing the ocean. This world, so much a part of me, will be farther and farther away until it disappears like a dream.

But fortunately, Sadik hasn't forgotten me. He seems to know when Mima is out of the house and no one else is around. In between my singing and playing the oud, he taps out a message on the wall. In a note he secretly passed to me one day when my sisters came home from school, he explained the secret code: One tap, *Beautiful*. Two taps, *Play that song again*. Three taps, *Play another song*.

I don't know why Sadik is so often home when I'm home. I hope he hasn't been punished too. Boys aren't punished as harshly as girls, so I hope that he is fine and that his bruise has healed.

A week before my departure, while Mima is out of the house, Sadik taps four times. I am not sure at first what that means. But then I realize it just means *open the door*, because I hear the knocks coming from our front door.

I open it a crack, and Sadik is standing there.

"I wanted to give you something," he whispers, and quickly hands me a letter before I close the door. Back in the bedroom I share with my sisters, I unfold the letter.

> *Dear Reina,*
> *I am so sorry that you are leaving. I wish I could go back in time and undo things, but that is impossible. You can't imagine how much I will miss you, but I hope you will be happy in Cuba. After you are gone, I think all I will dream about is leaving this place too and finding my luck somewhere else. Who knows? Life is full of surprises, and maybe we will meet again someday. I hope so! Mashallah. In the meantime, since we can't speak to each other, I'll keep listening to your beautiful music. I know when it stops, the silence will make me sad, as it will mean goodbye, or as you say in your language, adiós.*
> *Your friend,*
> *Sadik*

27

Take the Key

The morning that seems like it will never arrive finally does.

While my sisters are at school, I go into the bedroom I've shared with them our whole lives and look around at the bed, the dresser, the floor, the ceiling. Once we were three girls, three sisters. Now I will be gone, and there will just be two girls, two sisters. I imagine Suzi and Dina continuing to share the room until one of them marries. I won't be there to help Mima make lace for their wedding veils.

I pick up my trunk, filled with just the few clothes I own, take one last look, and whisper a prayer into the air. "Be a good house to my family, protect them from ill fortune, keep them safe."

Mima is in the courtyard waiting for me, and of course Papa is not present. Suzi and Dina haven't returned yet. I worry I won't get to see them before I leave. But just as I step outside, they come racing into the courtyard, their cheeks flushed.

"I'm glad we made it! But I had to rush Dina to go faster!"

Suzi says, and Dina replies, "That's not true! I outran you!"

I feel so old around them now. They sound so childish and innocent, and I think that I will even miss their quarreling.

"Little sisters, be well," I say as I pull them in for a three-way hug.

"Come back soon!" Suzi says.

"And bring us dresses and ribbons from Cuba!" Dina adds.

"And shoes to match!" Suzi exclaims.

"I'll need another trunk!" I tell them.

We laugh and enjoy being silly so as not to cry.

Then Mima comes over to hug me and says, "I want you to take the oud."

"No, Mima, it is so precious to you. How could I take your oud?"

Mima insists and brings it out to me. "It will make me feel better, knowing the oud is with you. And—" She puts something cool in the palm of my hand. "Here, Reina, take this extra key to remember that this will always be your first home in the world. Whenever you feel lost in Cuba, touch the key, and it will remind you that we are still here and we love you."

Mima and I hug each other and wipe away our tears. "Adio, adio kerida," she says, just like in the song she's taught me.

Adio, adio, kerida . . .
Va, buskate otro amor
aharva otras puertas . . .

Goodbye, goodbye, dear love . . .
Go, search for another love
knock on other doors . . .

Somehow, I leave my home, crossing through the courtyard, going out into the street.

I find Tía Zimbul waiting there with a man she has hired to transport us to the seaport.

"Ready?" she asks.

No words come to me. I feel like weeping and focus on holding the oud tightly under my arm.

The familiar street looks blurry, as if it's already turned into a memory.

I want to turn and have a last look at my home, but Tía Zimbul warns me, "Don't look back or you will turn to salt and never be able to start a new life in Cuba."

I listen to Tía Zimbul and don't look back.

28

Throw Your Oud Into the Sea

Am I awake or dreaming? I feel so lost as I accompany Tía Zimbul on our journey. A journey that would be exciting if I weren't taking it against my will.

We take the ferry from Silivri to Istanbul.

From there we travel by ship to Marseilles.

Then we cross France by train and journey to St. Nazaire.

We board the steamship *Cuba* of the Compagnie Générale Transatlantique.

We make a brief stop in La Coruña, Spain, where we are enchanted to hear the Spanish language. It is not the same as our old Spanish, but close enough that we can understand it.

And then we sail on to Cuba.

On board the ship, Tía Zimbul becomes seasick. I bring her clean water to drink and toasted bread to eat, and she can only take small bites. She can't leave her bed, so I wash her and her bedclothes and empty her chamber pot. I worry for her as well as for myself. How would I manage alone?

All week long my aunt drifts in and out of sleep. I stay

at her side, singing Spanish songs and playing the oud to comfort her.

During a nightmare, she calls out, "Rafi, Rafi!" And I remember my sweet cousin who died at war and never returned, Tía Zimbul's poor son without a tomb.

"Tía, don't worry. Rafi knew how much you loved him," I tell her. "He is resting in peace."

And she falls asleep again.

Two days before landing in Havana, she finally feels better. She's still weak and tired, but she can stand and walk a few steps. That afternoon, Tía Zimbul clutches my arm as we step out and stand on the deck. We gaze at the sea, which is the calmest it's been, and at last that dark shadow that's been following me since I left home fades away, and I'm no longer afraid. I even feel happy as I imagine setting foot in a new city and having adventures unlike anything I've experienced.

But then Tía Zimbul brings me back down to earth when she says, "You sing very well, Reina. You play the oud very well too. But remember it was your singing and your playing that got you into trouble. May El Dio forgive me for saying this . . . but for your own good, why don't you throw your oud into the sea and leave all that mournful music behind?"

I'm shocked that Tía Zimbul can think such a thing! How am I supposed to toss away the songs our ancestors passed on to us from the time they fled Spain? Or the oud that belonged to one of them?

"I can't do what you ask, Tía. The songs are part of me; they are in my blood. And the oud was a gift from Mima."

"Well, at least leave behind that stubborn and melancholy girl who you were in Silivri. Pretend she never existed. Start over in Cuba."

"I want to start over, but I'm sorry, Tía. I am who I am, and the songs and the oud must come with me."

29

The Breezes Are Soothing, Morning and Night

Tía Zimbul and I go to live in a run-down three-story building on Calle Oficios—a street overlooking the port of Havana. Our apartment consists of a living room with a coal stove and a bedroom. We are glad to have a bathroom, even though we share it with our second-floor neighbors, which is at least better than the chamber pots we had in Silivri. And we are fortunate to have a balcony. We can look out at the sea and watch the ships and ferries coming in and out of the port and gaze at the sailors stretching their legs as they walk on land again.

The breezes are soothing, morning and night, and so warm they remind me of those last hugs I received from my sisters and dear Mima.

I will never know where Papa was that day when I left Silivri. Since I was dead to him, he didn't need to say goodbye. I try not to think about this so much.

I write a letter to Suzi and Dina and Mima to tell them I am well and wish that they are too. I hope they will receive it and pray they will send me a reply. I dare not ask about

Sadik; I know that would cause trouble, but I hope he is well too.

In my loneliest moments, I reach into my pocket, where I keep the key Mima gave me to our house in Silivri. She said if I ever felt lost in Cuba to touch the key, and it would lead me back to my first home in the world, and so that's what I do, and the memories come flooding back—Mima teaching me Spanish songs, Suzi and Dina cuddling on either side of me in our bed, and Papa smiling, before he was angry with me, when I was his eldest and beloved child.

A sea separates me now from all that, a vast blue sea I cannot cross.

While my only family here is Tía Zimbul, there are several people from Silivri living in the building. You hear them speaking our old Spanish, though a few have been in Cuba long enough that now their Spanish sounds more like that spoken on the island.

Sometimes our Cuban neighbors wrinkle their foreheads in surprise when we speak. "Where are you from?" they'll ask, and when we say "Turquía," it's unbelievable to them. "We didn't know they spoke Spanish in Turkey," they'll say, and then, to avoid explaining too much, we reply, "It's Spanish from long ago, de munchos anyos. Our ancestors brought it from Spain to Turkey."

Our Cuban neighbors are friendly and invite us to their parties and ceremonies, but my aunt says I am not to go inside any of their apartments. I often hear drumming and dancing and singing that goes on for hours. How I wish I could join them and taste a bit of their happiness.

"Ven, niña," they say, and try to give me a plate of food that smells delicious, but I smile and shake my head, and they look at me with kindness and say not to be afraid—"no tengas miedo."

It's not them I'm afraid of—it's Tía Zimbul. Will she kick me out and leave me in the street if I misbehave? I don't want to find out.

30

She Is a Melancholy One, Isn't She?

And then Moshico, the man I am meant to marry in three years, comes to see me.

He pounds on the door, and as soon as Tía Zimbul opens it, he rushes in.

"Where is she? The girl who is to be my bride?" he demands. "Why have you waited so long to tell me she is here?"

"I sent word to you as soon as I could," Tía Zimbul replies. "I wanted Reina to have time to rest after the long journey. Surely you understand."

I am ironing Tía Zimbul's dresses, and even though I'm standing near the balcony to get fresh air, I'm sweating. I set the iron down and wipe my brow with my handkerchief, waiting for Tía Zimbul to tell me what to do.

"Please sit down," Tía Zimbul says to Moshico.

We only have two wobbly chairs that came with the apartment, along with the two narrow beds we sleep on.

Moshico doesn't sit down. Instead he opens his arms

and says, "Come, my bride, let me have a better look at you."

I inch away from the balcony and stand before him. He is handsome, with sharp, chiseled features, and his skin is dark from the sun. He is maybe fifteen years older than I am.

"You are younger than I expected. Look at that baby fat on your arms," he says, and he laughs.

I keep my head bowed, not knowing if I should speak.

"What do you have to say to me?" he asks.

I am shaking with fear but remember the words that Mima told me to say. "Thank you for accepting me as your bride. I will try to make you happy, when you take me as your wife when I turn fifteen."

"Why do you have such a sad face? You should be happy now. No need to be shy with me."

He opens his arms again, and I let him embrace me.

Tía Zimbul takes pity on me. "She is young, Moshico. And she is tired. She had to nurse me on that long journey across the sea. I was so sick I wasn't sure I'd make it. But now we are settling in, and Reina cooks wonderfully. She will make you borekas and bulemas like no one else, and she cleans and scrubs with determination and will take excellent care of your house and your children, when they come one day, mashallah, God willing."

I can't help it. I start to cry.

"She is a melancholy one, isn't she?" Moshico says,

shaking his head. "Tell me: What would make you feel better?"

"I wish my father would forgive me. He said I was dead to him. And nothing has ever hurt so much as that."

"My bride, you be good these next three years, wash and iron my clothes and fix me Shabbat dinner on Fridays, and after we marry, I will write to him and tell him to forgive you. How does that sound?"

"Thank you."

"I may seem gruff, but it's because I'm exhausted. I work very hard. It is summer here all year round, but it's not so easy to make a living. I peddle on the streets of Havana all day, and at night the only thing I want is to rest and go to sleep. But I will never abandon you. I know you have no other family here apart from your aunt."

"Thank you."

"You don't have to keep thanking me. Let's hope we come to love each other."

Then Moshico sees the oud resting on the edge of my bed.

"And look at that. You have brought an oud with you."

I smile at Moshico. To show him I will be a good wife, I say, "I will sing for you when we are married. I know many of the old Spanish songs."

"Perhaps. But sing all you can now, because you will probably be too busy taking care of our family when we marry," he replies. "Your oud can hang from a nail on the wall so you will remember your youth."

Before Moshico leaves, he passes Tía Zimbul some money.

"Have a new dress made for my bride; she's outgrown the one she's wearing," he says, and rushes off.

"What a good man Moshico is!" Tía Zimbul exclaims once we're alone. "Now I'll go have tea with the other Turkish ladies, and you can rest, my dear niece. I'm sure you're tired."

Watching the sky turn pink at the end of the day, I sit on the balcony and sing the song that brought me to Cuba, strumming on Mima's oud.

En la mar hay una torre ...
In the sea there is a tower ...

Like the girl in the song, I feel like I am trapped in a tower as I look down at the sailors. Maybe one of them will hear my song and come release me?

How many girls like me, through the ages, have sung these sad songs as they dreamed of freedom?

PART THREE

Alegra
1961

31

I Have Tasted Mamá's Tears in the Food I Eat

"¡Ay, no! ¡Ay, no! ¡Ay, no!"

Mamá lets out a wail that I can hear as I am huffing and puffing up the tall staircase to our apartment after returning home from school.

She often cries silently, letting the tears slide down her face, not bothering to dry them as she stirs a pot of lentil soup or kneads the dough for potato-and-cheese borekas. I have tasted Mamá's tears in the food I eat.

But this wail is like a clap of thunder. A dark cloud inside Mamá seems to have burst.

By the time I step inside, she has grown quiet. The balcony door is open, as always, to let in the air, and I can hear the distant echo of the waves. I wonder how many people heard Mamá. Couples strolling outside on the Malecón might have turned their heads our way. Maybe the sailors on the docks heard it too.

As usual, I'm alone with Mamá, since my two brothers and my sister, who are much older than me, now live with families of their own. And Papá is out playing dominoes after a day of work selling men's shirts door-to-door.

"Mamá, what happened? Tell me. Why did you scream like that? You scared me."

She's holding a letter in her hand—one of the letters she receives every now and then from her sisters in Turkey—and now she is mumbling, "My Mima, dear Mima, why couldn't you have waited a little longer so I could see you again?"

And that's how I learn that her mother, Mima, the grandmother I will never know, has died.

"I'm sorry, Mamá." I hug her, feeling her wet cheeks. "Tell me what it says in the letter."

I know so little about my mother's past. Every time a letter arrives from her sisters, Suzi and Dina, she reads it over and over, cherishing every word. But when I ask about her life in Turkey and why only she came to Cuba, all she'll say is that she was sent here when she was twelve to be her aunt's companion.

"Come, let's sit on the balcony. It's time I tell you more," she says.

It's late in the afternoon, and the sun is fading. We hear the mournful horn of the lanchita, the ferry that goes back and forth from Havana to Regla, as it sets off yet again across the harbor.

Mamá turns to me and says, "When I left Silivri, I always thought I'd get to go back to visit my family one day. And even though your papá and I only make enough money to live day to day, I never lost hope. But now she's gone."

"Why didn't your family come with you to Cuba? Tell me, Mamá. Did you come all by yourself?"

"I traveled here with Tía Zimbul—to this very apartment. Then, after I married your papá, she stayed with us till she died, right before you children were born."

"You've never told me how you met Papá. How did you decide to marry him?"

"I didn't decide. My father decided."

"What? I don't understand."

"It was an arranged marriage. I had no say in it. I didn't meet your father until I arrived in Cuba."

"Mamá . . . you didn't marry Papá when you were only twelve? That's my age!"

"No, hijica. He agreed to wait until I was fifteen."

"Oh, Mamá, that's so young! And I can't believe you didn't get to decide for yourself if you wanted to marry."

"Things were different when I was young. Arranged marriages weren't such an unusual thing back then."

She looks down at the letter in her hand, runs a finger across the Turkish stamps.

Then she continues, "What was sad was that my father stopped talking to me before I left Turkey and hasn't written a word to me since. Your papá tried to smooth things out with him. He wrote and told him what a good wife I was, but it was useless. He refuses to forgive me.

He's still alive in Silivri—would you believe it? He is twenty years older than dear Mima. How is it possible that she died first?"

"Mamá, what did you do to make your father so angry?"

"It was all because of a song, Alegra. If I hadn't wanted to sing it so much one night long ago, perhaps I'd still be in Turkey."

32

I Imagine Her Heart Traveling

Mamá walks down the entry hall of our apartment to where a musical instrument that looks like a guitar with a round belly has always hung on the wall. She takes it down and says, "Mima gave me this oud as a parting gift when I left Turkey. It's been gathering dust ever since I married your father. But now I'll sing a song for you that my mother and I loved. The song that caused me so much trouble."

She sits looking out to the sea and strums the oud lightly as if it were fragile. The sound of the oud rises into the air, and her eyes take on a faraway gaze as she sings:

En la mar hay una torre ...
In the sea there is a tower ...

As soon as she finishes singing, I tell Mamá, "That was so beautiful! But how did that song get you in trouble?"

Mamá sighs. "It happened on the evening Turkey celebrated its independence. I snuck out to celebrate and took my mother's oud. When my father found out I had been at a party with a group of boys, and even sang for them, he thought the worst of me. It was a different time back then. Girls hardly ever went out alone. My father said I brought shame on the family, and so he sent me to Cuba to eventually marry me off to your papá. And here I am."

"That's so sad, Mamá. But at least you got to have me!"

My comment makes Mamá smile, which is what I hoped.

"It's funny you sang Spanish songs, since you were from Turkey," I say. "Why was that?"

"It's because we originally came from Spain—long, long ago. Our ancestors were forced to leave during the Spanish Inquisition because they were Jewish. But we never forgot our Spanish roots. And our songs helped us hold on to the memory of the home we lost."

"So, Mamá, you were born in Turkey, but you felt Spanish? Just like I was born here in Cuba but feel like I'm Turkish too?"

"In a way, yes. I loved Turkey! And now I love Cuba."

"Well, speaking of Cuba, there is something I have to tell you."

Mamá brings her hand to her heart. "What is it, Alegra? What has happened?"

"Don't worry, Mamá. I am fine; everything is fine."

"So, what then?"

I take a deep breath. "I'd like to join the literacy campaign. I want to be a brigadista—to go teach people in the countryside how to read and write. There are posters all over town saying they need volunteers. And schools are closing soon in support of the revolution."

Mamá shakes her head. "Aren't you too young?"

"No! You only have to be ten years old, and I'm twelve."

"Are any of your friends from our Turkish circle volunteering?"

"None of them are interested. When I mentioned it to Leónora, she laughed, because she's such a city girl, and they need us in the countryside, where there may not be electricity or plumbing. Plus she said her family is thinking about moving to Miami. Lots of people are talking about leaving Cuba."

"Really? Leave Cuba?"

"That's what they're saying, Mamá."

"I suppose I should get out of the house more! I don't know any of the latest gossip."

"Well, now you know. But what do you think of my idea, Mamá? I think it'd be good for me to learn how to live off the land. The farmers in the countryside deserve an education too, right? Did you know that outside of Havana, there are hardly any schools? Imagine how sad you'd be if you couldn't read your sisters' letters and write back to them. We need to share the riches we have here in the city so all Cubans can live well."

"That's true, Alegra. You remind me of myself when I was your age. I wanted to be free so badly and hoped the new government in Turkey would make that possible. But then I was sent to Cuba . . ."

"I'm sorry, Mamá. But I'm glad you understand me."

I reach into my school bag and pull out the permission form. Only one parent has to sign, fortunately. "It'll be hard to be away from you, Mamá; that's the only thing that worries me. But will you let me go?"

Mamá stares into the distance, past the horizon, past where the sea meets the sky. I imagine her heart traveling all the way back to the home she left in Turkey, to the mother she wishes she could have seen one last time, the sisters who write her the letters she cherishes, the father who won't forgive her.

After a while, she says, "Yes, Alegra, you can go. And I will pray for you and keep the evil eye away."

"¡Gracias, gracias, gracias!" I throw my arms around her and feel her soft skin.

"Your father will be furious. We will have to keep it a secret until you leave."

"I know! Thank you again, Mamá."

Mamá lets go of me and reaches up to unfasten her gold necklace with the small Star of David on it. "Take this and keep it hidden under your clothes as I did. It was a gift from your father so I'd always remember I was Jewish."

"Won't Papá be upset that you're giving me the necklace he gave you?" I ask.

"Papá is not going to know about this either," she replies as she fastens it around my neck.

And as she says those words, Papá comes in the door.

33

Love on Shabbat

Mamá lights the Shabbat candles, and she and I recite the prayer. Then we sit down to dinner with Papá.

I feel the Star of David pressing into my skin. I don't touch it for fear Papá will notice.

Mamá has prepared a delicious array of Turkish dishes, which is her tradition on Friday to welcome Shabbat. Along with lentil soup and borekas, there is spinach with rice and lemon, fish cooked in a sauce of eggs and lemon, and what she calls *keftes*—little patties made of walnuts and leeks, fried in olive oil, served with stewed tomatoes and a sprinkling of lemon. Everything has lemon, which I love, and everything Mamá cooks tastes so good!

Then for dessert, there is Mamá's famous baklava, dripping with honey. Mamá often makes a big batch of the diamond-shaped pastry to share with the neighbors in our building, who all love it.

Now, as we eat dinner, the air grows tense with Papá's silence. Usually, he's happy on Friday nights and enjoys Mamá's dinner, but not lately, since his business is so bad.

Suddenly, he puts down his fork and exclaims, "I don't know what is going to happen to us. No one has money to buy things since the rebels took over. They came down from the Sierra Maestra mountains, promising to help the poor, but they're actually making us poorer! We'll have to keep living on the bit of savings we've stashed under the mattress and see how long it lasts. And I'll have to keep rummaging at the farmers market to find what food we can afford."

"As long as there is honey for the baklava, there will be sweetness in our lives," Mamá replies. "Remember, Moshico, a cruel dictator ruled Cuba before. Now there is hope for a better future. We just have to be patient. Things can't change that quickly."

Papá finishes eating his slice of baklava before he says, "I think you are mistaken, Reina. But your baklava is as wonderful as always." Then he gives Mamá a puzzled look. "Why aren't you wearing the necklace I gave you?"

What sharp eyes he has! He must have noticed that Mamá left open the top button of her blouse.

Mamá calmly replies, "Alegra admired my necklace, and I told her it was your gift to me. She is doing so well in school, I wanted to reward her. I hope you don't mind that I gave it to our daughter."

"I see," Papá says as he gets up. "Let's hope we don't have to sell that necklace to put food on the table!"

He goes to the bedroom to change into his one good suit

to go pray at the synagogue on Calle Inquisidor, as he does every Friday night.

"Here, let me get your things," Mamá says, and follows him. I watch as she finds the embroidered velvet pouch where he keeps his kippah and tallit in the dresser next to their bed, and she passes it to him, a sweet gesture I've observed for as long as I can remember. He, in turn, kisses her forehead and whispers, "You be good, mi Reina, be good," and she says, "I will."

It makes me happy to see them being kind to each other. After so many years together, I think Mamá has come to love Papá, maybe more than she realizes.

34

Baklava and Batá Drums on Calle Oficios

As Mamá and I clean up the kitchen, we hear the sounds of drums and dancing start up in the apartment above us, where my neighbor Teresita lives. Teresita's my age, but she goes to a neighborhood school, while I go to a Jewish school, so we only get to see each other in the building. The families in our building are a mix of Sephardic Jews from Turkey and Afro-Cubans, and Teresita's family is Afro-Cuban. Her parents are always friendly and have invited us to their celebrations many times, but Mamá and Papá never want to go.

"Mamá, please can we go upstairs tonight?" I ask. "Just for a little while. Teresita and her family are good neighbors, and they always invite us. Isn't it rude not to go?"

"All right, just for a few minutes," Mamá says, surprising me with her answer. My mother's been surprising me all day, and it feels like a veil's been removed and I'm finally getting to know her.

Teresita hugs me as soon as she sees us at the doorway. Her mother, Caridad, smiles and says to Mamá, "At last you've come, Señora Reina! We are so glad you could join us."

"It's a pleasure, Señora Caridad. Thank you for inviting us."

"And thank you for always sharing your delicious baklava with us."

"Well, here's some more!" Mamá says, passing her a tray.

"How nice! We will enjoy it! Now, do come in."

The apartment is filled with people. I recognize many of our neighbors swaying to the beat of the three batá drums, large, medium, and small.

Playing the large drum is Teresita's father, Carlos. Another neighbor plays the medium drum. And a boy who looks about my age is playing the smaller drum.

Teresita whispers, "That's my cousin Rolando. He's visiting from Santa Clara. My father is teaching him how to drum."

"I wish I had cousins here," I tell Teresita. "Mine are in Turkey, and I've never even met them."

"That's too bad! I get to see Rolando a lot. But I was worried we wouldn't be able to have our fiesta tonight. The rebels want us to believe in the revolution, not God and the saints. But we think we can support the revolution and still hold on to our customs."

Teresita has told me before that their ceremonies honor saints from West Africa, where her ancestors came from. Songs are sung in Lucumí, which comes from the Yoruba language.

I think of Papá at temple chanting prayers in Hebrew and Mamá memorizing the Spanish songs her mother passed down to her. I like that we each honor our ancestors in our own way. After listening to the drums for a while, Mamá and I can't help but sway to the rhythm.

When the drummers take a break and Mamá is talking with some neighbors, Rolando comes over and says hello.

Teresita introduces us, and Rolando says, "I like your name, Alegra."

"Thanks—my mother chose it because she hoped my life would be full of happiness."

"We could all use more happiness," Rolando says. "You look happy now. I hope you'll always be."

"Here's to happiness for us—and for all Cubans!" I say, hoping the revolution really will make things better for everyone.

"I'm glad we went," I tell Mamá once we return home.

"I am too, hijica. We must respect all religions. You know, when I was a girl in Turkey, we had Muslim neighbors. They had three sons, the same ages as me and my sisters, and I was very good friends with the oldest boy, Sadik. He's the one I was with that evening when I got into trouble. My sisters told me he left Turkey, but no one knows where he's gone. I wonder what happened to him."

We sit on the balcony, waiting for Papá to return from his prayers, and Mamá turns away wistfully and looks out to the sea as if the sea could give her the answer.

35

One Less Secret

Sunday afternoon, my brothers, León and José, and my sister, Flora, come over with their families.

Each of my siblings have two sons. José's children are still babies, but León's and Flora's boys are only a few years younger than me. It's funny I'm their aunt when they're almost my age, but I do my best to act grown-up around them. I don't roll on the floor or run around the apartment playing tag. I do sit at the table with the grown-ups, and listen to the conversation.

Mamá serves potato borekas and spinach bulemas, and there's just enough food for us all to have one helping. When the boys ask for more, Mamá says, "I'm sorry, hijicos, that is all we have. But I made bizkochikos for you. Would you like some?"

"Yes, yes, yes," the boys say, grabbing big handfuls, happy again.

Papá complains, "No one is buying my shirts. We are running out of money."

León, the oldest, exclaims, "Cuba is falling apart. Fidel Castro and his rebels are destroying the country! Fidel said he would return power to the people, but instead his government is snatching up everyone's private property. On Friday, while I was attending to a customer at the shoe store, the militiamen came and told my boss that he'd have to turn in the key to his store by the end of the week. If he doesn't, they'll take it by force. Everything belongs to the revolution now. But what's the revolution? Just the people in power!"

Flora chimes in. "I hear they're going to close all the religious schools, and synagogues and churches too."

Then José says, "That's not the worst of it. They say Fidel Castro plans to send the children to Russia to learn to be good communists! Can you imagine?"

To this, Flora replies, "We don't know if that's just a rumor. What we know for sure is they're sending children to the farthest corners of Cuba to teach the peasants how to read and write. Have you seen all the signs recruiting volunteers for their literacy campaign?"

Mamá and I remain silent, even though I'd like to ask what they think is wrong with promoting literacy. Neither of us dare to even glance at each other, afraid we'd give away the secret we're keeping from our family.

Papá shakes his head. "I've grown to love this island as much as Turkey, but who knows if we might have to leave one day?"

"People are already leaving," León says. "People from our Turkish circle. The ones with money are all going to Miami."

Mamá stares out at the sea listlessly, as she's been doing since she got word about her mother. Softly, she murmurs, "I received a letter from my sisters the other day with some sad news. My beloved mother, my Mima, has left the world. She died in Turkey."

"What?" Papá says. "Why did you not say anything before?"

"I was too sad to speak of it. Only Alegra knows, because she was here when I received the letter."

A cloud slides across the sky, blocking the sun. The blue sea turns sad and gray.

"I'm sorry, Mamá," Flora says.

"I am too," León says.

"And I," José adds.

Even my littlest nephews stop playing, alarmed at the news.

"After I left Turkey, I never saw her again," Mamá says. "El Dio must have wanted me to come here so I could have all of you, my dear family. But it is difficult being apart from my family in Turkey for so long. I always hoped to go back. But now my mother, my dearest Mima, won't be there . . ."

Fearing Mamá will start to cry, I blurt out, "Play the oud, Mamá. Sing one of the old Spanish songs your Mima taught you. That will make you feel better."

Papá is so shocked he jumps to his feet as if he's been

struck by lightning. "What are you saying, Alegra? Your mother hasn't played the oud since she married me."

"That is right, Moshico. And I doubt I'd remember how to play it anyway."

"Yes, I was just curious about it hanging on the wall . . . Mamá told me yesterday that it had been a gift from her mother—the last thing she gave her. I'm sad I never got to meet my grandmother. It'd be nice for Mamá to remember her by playing the oud."

"I suppose that would be all right, then," Papá says.

I smile at Mamá, and our gazes meet. We both breathe a sigh of relief. One less secret!

36

Enjoy Your Freedom

Early the next morning, Papá leaves to go peddling, and I quickly gather together the few things I'm bringing on the trip.

I give Mamá a hug, my eyes filling with tears. I'll miss her so much. And I worry that it'll be hard to calm Papá when he learns she gave me permission to join the literacy campaign.

"Don't cry, hijica," she says. "Enjoy your freedom."

"Gracias, Mamá. I hope Papá won't be too angry."

"Don't worry, I can handle him. And you know he doesn't stay angry for long."

"Thankfully, that is true, Mamá. Please tell him I am just trying to help people."

She comes to the door of the apartment to see me off, and I wave to her as I turn to go down the stairs. When I reach the landing, I hear someone else coming down from above. It's Teresita. Like me, she wears a loose blouse and pants and carries a small bag.

"Alegra, is it possible? Are you also volunteering to be a brigadista?" Teresita asks.

"I am."

"I'm so glad! I don't know anybody else who's going."

"Me neither. I'm so happy we can go together!"

We step out of the building, and I look up and see Mamá standing on the balcony waving a handkerchief to me.

I wave back. Then I take a deep breath. "Ready?" I ask.

Teresita's father, Carlos, suddenly emerges from the building.

"My father is a little overprotective." She turns to me with a smile. "He's escorting me to the Parque Central. Now he can escort the two of us!"

He chuckles when he sees me. "Well, look at that—the Turkish girl is also going to teach people how to read and write. That's wonderful!"

Under the glow of a May morning, the three of us set off through the narrow streets of La Habana Vieja. Carlos seems to know everyone in the neighborhood and greets friends as they stroll past. When we reach Calle Obispo, the street fills with people walking in opposite directions, some to the Parque Central, some to the Malecón and the sea.

As we approach the bookstore La Moderna Poesía, I see a man shuffling toward me. He's sweating and carrying a heavy load on his shoulder. Then I realize it's Papá! He sees me in the same moment and is so surprised he drops the shirts he's carrying.

"Papá! Let me help you."

I bend to pick up the shirts, which have scattered all over the street.

"What are you doing here?" he asks.

He sees how I'm dressed, he sees the bag I'm carrying, and he sees I'm accompanied by Teresita and her father. "Wait! Don't tell me . . ."

There's no way to hide the truth from him. "Papá, I'm going to alfabetizar, to volunteer in the literacy campaign. Teresita, from our building, is going too. So I won't be alone. Isn't that good?"

"Buenos días," Carlos says politely, extending his hand, but Papá only nods, not having a hand free as he holds on to the bundle of shirts with both arms.

"You can't go!" he says. "You don't have my permission."

"Please, Papá. I'm not doing anything wrong. I just want to teach people in the countryside how to read and write. Haven't you always encouraged me to study?"

"You go home right now, Alegra. Do you hear me? I don't want you taking part in that campaign. Fidel Castro and the rebels want to indoctrinate you, turn all of you children against your parents. Then they'll send you to Russia, and we'll never see you again!"

People are walking by and overhearing our conversation. "Shh, Papá, don't talk so loud. We're in the street."

Carlos then says, "Señor Mizrahi, if you continue to speak against the revolution, I'm going to have to report you. Maybe you didn't know—I'm a miliciano. I work for the government. But because you're my neighbor and your wife is so kind, I'll let it go if you quiet down and go peacefully. I'm taking your daughter and my daughter to the bus. I'll make sure they get on safely and are well taken care of. Does that sound all right to you?"

Papá doesn't reply. He looks suddenly very old. He is almost seventy, my papá, and seeing the wrinkles on his brow caked with dust, I feel sorry for him. I know that, in his own way, he wants the best for me.

He edges closer so we won't be heard. "Hijica, you are too young to go alone," he whispers. "There will be boys . . . and no Jewish people. Who will look out for you?"

"I'll be fine, Papá. Don't worry," I whisper back. "I won't do anything to shame you, I promise."

Those last words seem to touch a nerve, and Papá says, "Hijica, be careful." Then, with his bundle of shirts, he disappears into the crowd.

37

As Cuban as the Palm Trees

We crowd into the buses and drive off in a caravan, passing fields of palm trees on a winding road so close to the sea it seems like we're almost riding on the water.

As I gaze out the window from my seat next to Teresita, I feel my heart beating with excitement and a tinge of fear. I've never been around so many exuberant young people of so many different backgrounds squeezed together. And I've never left Havana before.

Teresita has been looking out the window too, and she turns to me. "The palm trees are so tall and majestic, aren't they? As if they could touch the sky. No wonder they're called royal palms!"

"Our country is beautiful," I tell her. "This is the first time I am seeing it."

"I'm glad your father let you come," she says. "It's kind of funny—your father didn't want you to join the literacy campaign because he doesn't like the rebels, and my father insisted I join because it looks good for him, since he supports the rebels. I don't know which is better or worse. Do you?"

"I see what you mean. We want to make our own choices, but they want us to do what's best for them. In the end, they're not so different from each other."

"Not at all."

She reaches into her bag and takes out a small plaster statue of a Black woman dressed in a long blue robe. "My father gave me this. It's the Virgin of Regla, also called Yemayá. She's the goddess of the sea and mother of all living things. Even though Papá is a miliciano and is supposed to believe in the revolution, he still believes in Yemayá, and I do too. I pray Yemayá will bring me home safely."

"I understand, Teresita. I have the Jewish star here on my necklace. My father gave it to my mother, and she gave it to me, to keep me safe."

I show the star to her before hiding it under my blouse again.

"It's so pretty how the gold gleams. And you hide it, just like I hide my Yemayá. We don't want to call attention to ourselves, right? After all, we're part of the revolution now!"

She winks at me, and I know from that moment that I can trust Teresita with everything.

"Teresita, I'm glad I'm not going alone to the literacy campaign. It's nice to be going with you."

"I'm glad I'm going with you too, Alegra. It's a little intimidating being around so many older kids. We can stick together."

When the caravan of buses pulls up at Varadero Beach, all of us are delirious with joy. Our first stop is at the island's famous beach resort! Who knew we'd be treated so well! The town is filled with luxury hotels that were built for American tourists. They used to come in droves before the triumph of the revolution. Now the tourists are gone. Varadero, we learn, has been turned into a training camp for us brigadistas who will teach the poor to read and write.

Everyone cheers as we step off the bus and gather around to wait for instructions. Some of the girls and boys break out in a cha-cha dance, locking arms, singing, "¡Viva la revolución! ¡Viva!"

The literacy leaders, three men and one woman, decked out in their green uniforms and boots, arrive in a jeep and calmly hop down and come over to greet us. "¡Muy bien, muy bien!" they say, glad to see so much enthusiasm for the revolution.

But once they announce that girls and boys will be housed separately, the singing and dancing stops.

"Please, can't we be together?" a few of them shout.

One of the leaders, a man with a stern gaze, tells them, "No. This is a serious mission. It's not the time to be looking for girlfriends and boyfriends. We're going to train you to be brigadistas."

And without any more discussion, they break us up into two groups and take the boys to Camp Granma and the girls to Kawama.

Teresita and I ask to stay together, and the woman from the FMC, the Federation of Cuban Women, who is arranging all the accommodations, says that's fine. She's an elegant woman. Though she's wearing the uniform and boots, her fingernails are painted bright red, and her blond hair is styled in a perfect flip as if she's just gone to the beauty parlor.

"You're very young, niñas. I'm surprised your families let you come."

Teresita hooks her arm around mine. "We're young, but we want to serve the revolution. And we're vecinas. We live in the same building on Calle Oficios."

"I see. You must come from humble families. It's unusual for white and Black girls to live in the same building in most of Havana, but in your neighborhood, people mix a little more."

"She's not a white girl," Teresita replies, smiling at me. "She's turca. Her family came from Turkey."

"But I was born here in Cuba," I quickly reply. "I'm as Cuban as the palm trees, as José Martí would say."

The woman laughs. "You're both very sweet. We're glad to have such dedicated young revolutionaries among us. I'll keep an eye on you and make sure you stay together and don't get sent too deep into the countryside. If you need anything, my name is Carmen."

That night I lie in a cot in a room filled with dozens of girls. They're only interested in talking about boys and giggling. I'm relieved when they finally fall asleep.

But then I toss and turn. I'm thinking of Papá this morning as he walked away with his bundle of shirts. I hope he's all right. And Mamá too. I clasp the star on my necklace and tell myself we'll all be fine, but I still feel afraid.

Teresita's cot is next to mine. "Are you awake?" she whispers.

"I am."

"I thought so."

She reaches out her hand and I take it, and soon we both close our eyes and let ourselves dream.

38

Holding Up Our Books

Every day, Teresita and I tell ourselves we'll try to get to the beach, but there's never enough time. The leaders keep us busy with lessons and lectures.

We all get a teachers' manual, *Alfabeticemos*, that shows us how to teach our students to read. The letter *F* is for *Fidel*. The letter *Y* is for *Yanqui*, the Americans who are now our enemies because they want to bring down the revolution. And they give us another book, *Venceremos*, a primer for the students. It has chapters called "The Revolution," "Fidel Is Our Leader," and "The Land Is Ours." We're taught how to teach the students to write both print and cursive letters, how to sound out words from syllables, and how to create sentences by joining together verbs and nouns.

I keep wanting to pinch myself. Here I am, a twelve-year-old girl who's grown up in a crumbling building on Calle Oficios, and the revolution is training me to be a teacher! What could be bad about that? When I return home, I'll sit down with Papá and patiently tell him about the good things the revolution is doing for the Cuban people.

When they give us uniforms, socks, and boots, an olive-green beret, and a leather belt, Teresita and I are so excited! We change into our new outfits immediately and parade around feeling very grown-up and important.

Now we feel like real brigadistas in the Army of Literacy Teachers.

We receive pencils for our students and a satchel to carry our things. And they give us paper and stamps for writing home. I promise myself I'll write to Mamá and Papá as soon as I start teaching.

They even give us toothpaste and soap and teach us first aid.

We each get a hammock and a kerosene lantern too.

"There might not be beds for you in the homes of the campesinos. That's why you're getting hammocks," the leaders warn us. "And there might just be dirt floors."

"And what's the lantern for?" someone asks.

The leaders explain that many families don't have electricity and we may need to teach some of our classes in the evenings after they're done with the farmwork.

At the end of our training, they tell us that once our students learn to read and write, we must tell them to write a letter to Fidel, thanking him for everything they've learned through the literacy campaign. This letter will show just how well they've learned to read and write.

Finally, we're taught the hymn of the literacy campaign and told to sing it with feeling:

¡Cuba, Cuba . . . !
Con el libro en alto cumplimos una meta:
llevar a toda Cuba la alfabetización.
Por llanos y montañas
el brigadista va
cumpliendo con la Patria,
luchando por la paz.
¡Abajo imperialismo!
¡Arriba libertad!
Llevamos con las letras
la luz de la verdad.

Cuba, Cuba . . . !
Holding up our books, we fulfill our goal:
bring literacy to all of Cuba.
Along plains and mountains
we brigadistas go
loyal to our country
and fighting for peace.
Down with imperialism!
Up with liberty!
We carry with our words
the light of truth.

I fall asleep thinking how different this revolutionary song is from Mamá's Spanish song about the girl trapped in a tower at sea. And how, unlike Mamá, I'm getting to decide what I want to do with my life. Poor Mamá, how much she has suffered. Sent away from her family and promised to Papá when she was only twelve.

I'm so thankful for my freedom. And that I am able to fight for a cause I believe in.

39

A Man Who Can Make Us Shout Until We Have No Voice

I wake up to Teresita tapping me on the shoulder.

"Oh no, have I overslept?" I ask.

"Just a little, but you must have needed it. Now we have to get moving and pack up. Remember, it's our last day." Then she smiles. "And guess who's coming to see us off."

"Who?" I say, still groggy as I change into my uniform.

She makes a little leap into the air. "¡El Comandante! Fidel Castro himself!"

"What? Really? No, it can't be!"

"It's true. He'll be here soon."

"I can't believe it! That's going to be like seeing Superman or something."

"I know, I know. Come, let's go!"

It's burning hot outside. Our uniforms are made of thick cloth, and the boots are heavy. After a few steps, I feel beads of sweat starting to pour down my back. I can barely keep pace with Teresita. By the time we reach the outdoor stage, everyone is waiting under the bright sun—the girls in one group, the boys in another.

We see Carmen, and she waves to us. She has saved us a spot in the front.

Suddenly there he is . . . Fidel . . . so tall and sure of himself. Like a king.

Teresita gasps. "Alegra, I can't believe this is happening!"

We both jump and cheer along with the other young people in our group.

Fidel begins to speak, and his voice, so loud, so confident, sends a shiver up my spine.

"There would not have been a revolution if there had not been so much injustice against our people! The revolution was a necessity!"

We clap.

"We have decided to eliminate illiteracy in Cuba during this year. We know it is a difficult task. More than a million people over ten years of age do not know how to read and write. They must be helped! They must be persuaded that they can study. There can be no progress without education!"

We clap again.

He keeps talking, and I listen attentively at first, but after a while it's hard to concentrate with the sun scorching the top of my head. I hear the palm trees rustling in the breeze and the sea waves roaring, and I wish I could be bathing in the water.

"You are going to teach, but as you teach, you will also learn. You are going to learn much more than you can possibly teach . . . Because while you teach them what you have learned in school, they will be teaching you what they have learned from the hard life that they have led. They will teach you the 'why' of the revolution better than any speech, better than any book."

Fidel ends his speech, and we cheer and clap, now because it's over.

The older girls and older boys hold up giant balloon pencils, and they give us paper Cuban flags that we twirl around, shouting, "¡Cuba, Cuba, Cuba!"

Then everyone shouts, "¡Fi-del, Fi-del, Fi-del!"

We keep shouting his name until our throats are raw and sore.

At last, Fidel waves his hand as a sign for us to stop.

Carmen rushes over to us with a bouquet of orchids. "Alegra and Teresita, you're the youngest in our group. Go up to Fidel and give him these orchids. Say gracias for all of us."

Teresita grabs me by the elbow. "Come on, Alegra. Don't be afraid. He's a hero, but he's also human, just like us."

I wish I had wings to fly away. I'm afraid to come too close to a man who can make us all stand in the sun for hours, as he so effortlessly does, a man who can make us shout until we have no voice.

I let Teresita carry the orchids and follow her up to the stage, where Fidel waits for us, smiling and stroking his beard.

Teresita gives him the orchids, shakes his hand, and says gracias. Then she nudges me toward him, and I too shake his hand and say gracias.

He nods and smiles at us, and everyone cheers.

Then a photographer comes and snaps a picture of Fidel with us. A picture of me next to Fidel? I know Papá will be upset about that and hope he never sees it!

Carmen appears and walks straight over to Fidel, as if she's known him forever, and says, "Aren't these girls special? One Black, one white, and they live in the same building on Calle Oficios. As you can see, the extrovert is Teresita, and the shy one is Alegra, who's turca. Well, her parents are Turkish. She was born here in Cuba."

"Our revolution is for all Cubans, of whatever background." Fidel turns to me and smiles, and I have to lift my chin to look back at him because he's so tall.

Then he goes on to say, "But any traitors who want to bring down our revolution are gusanos. We don't need any of those worms here on our beautiful island, do we?"

I shudder at the way he says that word, *gusanos*, as if he knows that Papá has said nasty things about him and the rebels. But that's impossible! Or is it? What if Teresita's father reported Papá, the way he threatened to? To make that frightening thought go away, I bring my hand to my chest. There I feel the Jewish star on Mamá's necklace under my uniform, and I silently make a wish that Papá be safe.

Fidel watches me. "Well, do you agree that we don't need any gusanos here?"

"No, no, Comandante," I say breathlessly. "I mean, yes, yes, I agree, Comandante, we don't need them here."

He laughs boisterously. "Is it no or yes?"

Luckily at that moment other people crowd around, competing for a few minutes with Fidel, and he forgets about me.

Carmen comes and pulls us away. "Nicely done, niñas. You've behaved so well that I'm taking you to the beach. Go change. I'll get sandwiches and colas. Be ready in ten minutes!"

With that I put all thoughts of traitors and worms aside—finally, we are going to visit the beach!

40

Born on an Island

Carmen takes us to a beach with the most beautiful soft white sand and turquoise water.

Pointing to a mansion next to the sea, she tells us, "That's the du Pont estate. It's filled with precious woods and marble. The mansion belonged to a very rich family before the revolution. I hope we can turn it into a school now." She carefully tucks her perfectly curled hair into a swim cap and then says, "Well, niñas, tell me: Do you know how to swim?"

We both shake our heads no.

She laughs. "You two were born on an island, surrounded by the sea on all sides, and you don't know how to swim? We'll have to change that. Follow me. We'll wade in slowly, and then I'll teach you how to float. The water is nice and calm today."

It's low tide, and the water reaches up to our waists. I didn't know the sea would be so warm. We splash around for a while, and the fish dance at our feet.

Before coming to the beach, I took off my necklace with

the Jewish star and hid it in my satchel. It feels strange now, not wearing it, like I've lost Mamá and Papá and my ancestors. But of course I haven't!

I feel grateful that Mamá and Papá will be waiting for me in Havana when I return in a few months. Perhaps Papá will be a little angry with me, but his mood will pass as it always does. That's one thing we can count on with my father.

I set aside my thoughts and worries when Carmen begins to show us how to float. She stretches out on her back with her arms open wide and stands by each of us as we do the same.

"The trick is to stay relaxed," she says. "On a calm day like this there are no riptides to be concerned about. Just look up at the sky, and the water will keep you afloat. Don't be afraid. I won't let you girls drown!"

We gradually get the hang of it. Soon Teresita and I can float easily, and we're eager to learn how to swim. Carmen tells us to turn onto our stomachs, and she holds our bellies up in the water as we make our first efforts to kick our feet and propel ourselves forward with our arms.

We enjoy it so much. Neither of us want to get out of the water.

"You two were born to swim," Carmen says. "Perhaps you are part mermaid."

"I would have never dreamed of that until now," I tell Carmen. "I always thought the sea was something sad and scary, like an endless valley of tears—probably because my mother was forced to cross it and leave behind the family she adored. Now you've taught me that the sea can be a happy place."

"Just like your name," Teresita says, "full of happiness."

We stay in the sea for hours pretending we are mermaids, and when we finally come out, our skin is all wrinkly. It's like time has stopped, and we're island creatures returned to the sea where we belong.

41

Teach Us

"You both will be stationed in Melena del Sur," Carmen announces the next day.

Carmen says it's a safe location for young girls and isn't too far from Havana, only a few hours away. She doesn't want us to go to the mountains of the Sierra Maestra or the Escambray.

"It's too dangerous there," she tells us solemnly. "The counterrevolutionaries killed two brigadistas, and they have threatened to kill more."

Teresita and I try not to look scared. But I clutch at my necklace, and I see Teresita gripping the little plaster statue of Yemayá.

"I promise, you'll be fine," Carmen adds with a smile. Then she waves goodbye and says, "Take care, niñas. Be good!" as we are driven away in a government jeep.

The ride to the countryside is bumpy, but the scenery is pretty.

"Look at the fields planted with sugarcane!" Teresita says.

"Listen to the tree frogs!" I respond.

When we arrive in the town, our driver, Jorge, points out the pharmacy, the general store, and the movie theater where we'll have our meetings with the literacy leaders of the region.

Then Jorge drives down a small stretch of road and stops at the end, where there are two houses facing each other. Both are bohíos, simple wooden houses made with a thatched roof.

"This is it," he says.

People from each house—an older white couple and a Black family—come out to greet us, and Jorge introduces us. "These two girls are the brigadistas. They're going to live with you and teach you how to read and write."

The old woman has deeply lined, sunburned skin and wears a stained apron over her dress. She starts laughing. "How will these two teach us anything? They're not teachers. They're little girls dressed in trousers!"

"I think you might be surprised," Jorge tells them.

The Black couple nods politely, and the woman says, "Welcome, bienvenidas. We have no school here, so whatever you teach us about reading and writing will be more than we know."

Her husband adds, "We don't have the luxuries you have in Havana, but if you like the quiet, we have plenty of that."

Then their three young children, two boys and a girl, start chanting, "Please, please, please! Teach us, teach us!"

The old white man rubs his eyes and removes his torn-up

straw hat to get a closer look at me and Teresita. "I guess they think of everything," he says. "They sent a white girl and a Black girl."

This time I'm happy to see that Teresita doesn't try to correct the old man and tell him I'm not white but turca. Instead, she smiles and says, "The color of our skin may be different, but we're both as Cuban as the palm trees."

The old man responds, "Well then, bienvenidas, welcome, niñas. It's been a while since we've had any visitors here in the countryside."

As we gather our things from the jeep, Jorge tells us that Teresita's been assigned to live with the Black family, and I've been assigned to live with the white family. "This way everyone will be comfortable," he says.

Teresita whispers to me, "There's still so much prejudice in Cuba, and we've just had a revolution! Why do they assume Black people and white people need to have brigadistas of their same color?"

"You're right—it shouldn't be that way. Let's do things together as much as we can."

Teresita nods, then says, "Sure hope that old lady doesn't drive you nuts!"

"Don't worry. I can handle her. We'll show them we're great teachers! Melena del Sur will be the first territory where everyone is literate!" I say, repeating the slogan I learned at the training camp in Varadero.

"¡Sí!" Teresita agrees. "That's the spirit."

42

In a House With Total Strangers

I follow the old couple into their yard, where there's an outdoor cooking pit and a table and chairs under some trees.

"What kind of trees are they?" I ask.

The old woman smiles. "Can't you tell from their sweet smell? They're mango trees."

"I love mangos," I say. "How wonderful to have your own trees!"

"You'll have plenty of mangos to eat in a few months. But you'll have to help me gather them. My children and grandchildren have all moved to Havana," she says. "They left the two of us viejitos here in the countryside to fend for ourselves."

"Well, I am here and happy to help, compañera," I tell her.

We've been instructed to call the women by that word, to think of them as comrades, and to call the men compañeros. At the training camp they said the words *señora*, *señorita*, and *señor* separate people by age and status. Now, with the revolution, we are all equal.

The old woman smiles for the first time and tells me her name is Gloria López Rodríguez. "You don't need to call me compañera," she says. "Just call me Gloria."

"I will do that," I say. "Have you lived here a long time, Gloria?"

"I was born in this very house," she replies. "I will never leave. My roots are here."

Gloria shows me the house. It's hot and muggy outside, but the thatched roof keeps it cool indoors. They have two wooden rocking chairs. Their bed is on one side of the room, and Gloria says they can set up a cot in the corner for me.

"A cot will be good," I say politely. "I also have a hammock that I can set up outside."

"No, no, niña, you sleep in here with us. The hammock is fine for taking a siesta during the day, but at night it's better if you're inside, away from animals and bugs."

It's odd to think I will sleep in a house with total strangers, but Gloria does her best to make me feel at home, stuffing a threadbare pillowcase with mint and other herbs that she says are calming. And her husband, who tells me to call him Alfredo, says, "It's nice to have a young one with us again."

Later Gloria prepares a meal of roasted yuca, malanga, and plantains in the cooking pit, and we eat in the shade of the mango trees.

"It all tastes so fresh and delicious!" I say.

"Of course it does, niña. The vegetables were pulled out of the earth this morning."

I'm relieved I don't have to slyly remove garnishes of ham from my food, as I did at the training camp in Varadero, since Jews aren't supposed to eat pork.

As the sun begins to set, I help Gloria wash the dishes with the water she's collected in a bucket. There's a well nearby, she tells me, and tomorrow we'll go collect more water.

When the night turns velvety dark, Alfredo says, "You must see our stars," and he leads me and Gloria a few steps away from the trees. "You can see them much better here than in the city with all the streetlamps."

He's right. The stars glitter like sequins in the sky. "Qué bello," I say. "Muy bello."

The sky has never seemed so wide, the stars so close, my heart so filled with gratitude to all those who came before me and gave me life.

The house is pitch-dark when we return to it as there's no electricity, so I can barely see in front of me.

Alfredo says, "Sorry it's so dark, niña. Be careful where you step."

"That's what this lantern is for," I say as I find it in my bag and light it as I've been taught. Its brightness fills the room, and Gloria and Alfredo are so delighted they clap cheerfully.

With a chuckle, Alfredo says, "Look at that! How well they prepared you for a visit to the countryside."

"Don't stay up too late," Gloria tells me. "We wake up early here."

"I won't," I promise.

They go to sleep, and I go back outside with my lantern and sit at the wooden table to write a letter.

> May 8, 1961
>
> Dear Mamá and Papá,
> I hope you are both well. I am in Melena del Sur, which is not too far from Havana, and I am doing fine. Fortunately, I am here with Teresita, and we are staying with two different families who live next to each other. Tomorrow we will begin teaching them how to read and write. They think we're too young to teach them, but we plan to prove them wrong!
>
> Our literacy leader, Carmen, was really nice and helped prepare us for coming here. Before we left, we were given books to teach with and writing supplies. They even gave us each a small allowance in case we need to buy anything. Since there's nothing I need, I'm going to save it all and give it to you when I return, Papá, so don't worry if you aren't selling shirts. And, Mamá, I miss your cooking so much.
>
> The people hosting me are very friendly. We had roasted vegetables for dinner, and they have mango trees on their property, so I will be eating lots of those! And right now, I am writing this letter outside under the light

of a lantern. I have a cot to sleep in, but tomorrow I will set up the hammock they gave us at the training camp. I'll lie there and take my siestas beneath the sweet scent of mangos.

Please write to me here at Melena del Sur so I know you are well, and tell me about the family. How are my brothers and sister and nephews? I miss you all very much and remember you every day.

*With all my love,
your hijica Alegra*

43

The Well

I awaken at dawn to the crowing of the roosters instead of the sounds of Havana's noisy streets.

Gloria and Alfredo are outside drinking coffee.

"¡Buenos días!" I say as I pass them on my way to the barn where their two cows live. Gloria told me it was also a good spot to "use the bathroom." The other choice is to go in the open, past the yard, but you have to be careful not to be seen and not to get bitten by bugs. I've never liked sharing a bathroom with our neighbors on our floor on Calle Oficios, but in the countryside there's no bathroom at all! I'll have to get used to the earthy breath of the cows when I visit them.

"Here, wash up," Gloria says when I return, and she passes me a basin of water. I pull out the bar of soap I was given at the training camp, and she points to a corner of the house that has been turned into a small washroom.

I splash water on my face and then take a long look at myself in the cracked mirror on the wall. I seem more confident already, just from having spent a night on my own with strangers.

When I step back out, I sit down next to Alfredo, and he gives me a big smile.

Gloria serves me warm milk for breakfast. "Gracias, está muy rica," I say. "This is truly the most delicious milk I've ever tasted!"

Alfredo chuckles. "You've met La Linda and La Mariposa in the barn. You must thank them. They're the cows that are kind enough to give us their milk."

I never knew cows had names, but why not? Soon I'll get to know which one is La Linda and which La Mariposa.

"I'm ready to begin the first lesson whenever you, Alfredo, and you, Gloria, would like," I announce.

"There's much we have to do before we can sit and study," Gloria replies. "Let's get the chores done in the house and let Alfredo check on the corn and the sugar in the fields and take the cows and goats to pasture, and then we'll get started."

We were taught in the training camp to be respectful of our hosts and help them with their work. We're to learn from their lives too. And so I pass the day with Gloria, sweeping the floor and cleaning the house, washing the clothes, and feeding the chickens. The pig has its own barn, and we have to clean up the mess in there too. Gloria says they're saving the pig for their Nochebuena celebration at the end of the year. We'll be done with our teaching before then, so I'm glad I won't be expected to eat it.

After all that work, I'm exhausted, but then it's time to go to the well to collect water.

When we step out to the road with our water buckets, there is Teresita with her host mother and the children.

Teresita and I hug each other as if we've been separated for years.

"My, my, you two are such close amigas!" Gloria remarks. "Isn't that something?"

I introduce Teresita to Gloria, and Teresita introduces me to her host mother, Ramona. The children are sweet and are cutely named Pepo, Pepino, and Pepa. They've already taken a liking to Teresita and won't leave her side.

Even though Gloria and Ramona are neighbors, they act as if they barely know each other. But I suppose it's not so different from how my parents—especially my father—are with some of our neighbors.

We walk down the path to the well, the tree frogs chirping all around us.

Pepo, Pepino, and Pepa run about, calling out, "Mira, mira, mira, is that it, Mami?"

Ramona laughs and explains, "They're looking to see if they can spot a zunzuncito. You know what that is, don't you?"

"I know from schoolbooks that the zunzuncito is the tiniest hummingbird in the world, and it only exists in Cuba, but I've never seen one. Have you, Teresita?" I ask.

"No, I've never seen one either."

"Sometimes you can see a zunzuncito around here," Ramona says. "They're so small, the size of your thumb, such beautiful little things."

"I hope we get to see one!" Teresita and I both exclaim, making Gloria and Ramona laugh.

"They're little miracles," Gloria remarks, and Ramona says, "Yes, they are!"

When we get to the well, Ramona tells Gloria, "Please, you go first."

Gloria smiles. "It's fine, you go first; you have the children."

"We can wait," Ramona replies, also with a smile.

Maybe they're being polite because Teresita and I are there, but still it's nice to see them being considerate of each other. Even if they don't learn to read and write, if they only learn to be better neighbors, our stay will have been worth it. But I'm confident we'll teach them to read and write. I'm not going to disappoint Fidel! Or myself.

Teresita says, "Let's take turns. You fill a bucket, Gloria, then we fill a bucket, until we all have enough water."

Pepo and Pepino fill and carry a big bucket together, while little Pepa fills and carries a small bucket. Teresita and I have two big buckets each, and they're heavy and have to be carried slowly so as not to spill any of the precious water. Gloria and Ramona are each able to carry one bucket on their shoulder and another on their arm.

When we return to their houses, we all say goodbye.

"Teresita, hasta mañana."

"Alegra, hasta mañana."

44

And What Is That Star You Wear Around Your Neck?

I set up the hammock between the mango trees and urge Gloria to try it. She stretches out for a moment and then pulls herself up again. "This is relaxing, but I don't have time right now," she says. "You enjoy it, niña," she tells me, and insists I lie in it while she makes dinner. I close my eyes and soon fall asleep, napping under the mango trees, just as I said I'd do in my letter to Mamá and Papá. I only sleep for half an hour, but I awake refreshed, as if I've slept for days and days like in a fairy tale.

Alfredo returns home at dusk, carrying stalks of sugarcane and a sack of corn for the pig. We share another dinner of yuca, malanga, and plantains, and then he offers me some of the sugarcane. As I sit munching the sweet fibers, I fall into a hazy lull and almost forget I'm supposed to be teaching.

"Do you want to start learning how to read and write?" I ask.

"Of course," Gloria replies. "¡Claro que sí!"

It's dark by then and I light the lantern, and we all sit at the table. It feels strange that I will be the teacher of two elders who could be my grandparents, but I pull out the notebooks and pencils and write out the letters of the alphabet. We go over them slowly, one by one, just as I was taught to do at the training camp.

"Repeat after me," I say. "A, B, C..." And I point to the letters as we say them. When we get to the end of the alphabet, we repeat the letters a second and a third time. They do well, and we're ready to move on. Next, I'll teach them how to write their names, but first I have to teach them how to hold the pencil in their hands.

Gloria gets the hang of it right away. I hold my hand over hers to show her how to make the sweep of the G, and then the other letters come easily. She enjoys writing her name and fills the page with the word *Gloria*.

With Alfredo, I help him hold the pencil, but it keeps falling out of his hand. Both of his hands are like twisted tree limbs. His right hand is worse than the left, mangled into a knot.

"That's from all the years of cutting cane and working in the fields," he says. "I started as a little boy. My father wouldn't let me go to school; he said it was a waste of time. Now my hands are worthless, except to do the rough work I do here in the countryside."

I tell him, "It's all right, Alfredo. Please don't worry. I will teach you how to read. Reading is as important as writing."

I write out his name, letter by letter—*ALFREDO*—and

show him how to pronounce the vowels and the consonants.

"¡Ahora sí!" he exclaims when he finally understands how to read his own name, and Gloria and I clap for him. Then he brushes away a tear. "I thought I was a brute. Now I can at least read my own name."

"You'll soon be reading more, Alfredo. You are both catching on so fast!"

Alfredo smiles. "Come, little teacher, turn off that lantern now; it's time to admire the stars."

Once again we walk into the middle of the yard and gaze at the sky.

I realize it's Friday night. Shabbat has started. I instinctively touch the Star of David on Mamá's necklace, feel its points. I silently say the Jewish prayer we recite when we light the candles on Shabbat eve.

Then I hear Gloria saying, "I am glad you like the stars."

"I've never seen them shine so brightly."

"And what is that star you wear around your neck? I noticed it in the morning while you were sleeping."

I hesitate—not sure if I should tell Gloria and Alfredo that I'm Jewish.

A picture of the Virgin of La Caridad del Cobre hangs over their bed, and a picture of the Virgen de Regla hangs over my cot. I don't want them to think I'm any different from them by mentioning that I've been brought up in another religion.

"It's pretty." Gloria smiles and asks, "Was it a gift?"

"Yes, from my mother. And the star means I'm Jewish."

Alfredo looks confused. "But your friend said you are both as Cuban as the palm trees."

"Yes. I was born here in Cuba, but my mother and father were born in Turkey, and our family originally came from Spain. Our ancestors were forced to leave Spain, long ago, because they were Jewish."

"That's very sad, but don't worry about anything like that happening in Cuba. We don't kick people out here," Alfredo responds.

"And soon, maybe religions won't divide us so much," Gloria says. "I only keep my religious pictures on the wall because they were my mother's. I have a lot of respect for las virgencitas, but I know I'm meant to hang up the picture of Fidel that they gave us at that meeting about the revolution. As Fidel says, it's not saints and spirits but literacy and education that will bring progress to our country. Isn't that right, maestra?"

I nod and feel touched at how earnestly she calls me maestra, but her words make me nervous too. Will we have to put up a picture of Fidel in our house—not because we want to, but because we're expected to? And will I have to give up wearing my Jewish star?

45

Zunzuncito

As the days and weeks pass, Teresita and I get into the routine of helping our host mothers with all the chores and then meeting in the afternoon to bring back water from the well. Pepo, Pepino, and Pepa always come with us and keep us entertained on the walk with their search for the zunzuncito. Even if we'll never get to see one, the pleasure of looking for the littlest hummingbird in the world is fun enough.

Our arms are stronger as we walk back with our buckets of water. We are able to lift them higher and not spill a drop.

At night I continue my classes with Gloria and Alfredo, and I'm proud of my two students! They can recognize so many words now and are eager learners. Gloria's goal is to read the newspaper, and Alfredo surprises me when he says, "What I wish is to be able to read José Martí's poems. Show me how to read *Yo soy un hombre sincero / de donde crece la palma*. That's who I am, a sincere man from where the palm trees grow."

"I'll be happy to write that verse down for you, Alfredo, so you'll learn to read it."

"Gracias, mi vida," he says, and the sweetness of his voice, like the sugarcane he's given me to taste, fills me with happiness.

Teresita's family is learning quickly too. She has taught Ramona, her husband Francisco, and all three children how to write their names. Pepo, Pepino, and Pepa have lots of questions about everything. They are fascinated by history, and before bedtime, Teresita reads to them from the *Venceremos* primer, with its chapters on Fidel Castro and the revolution.

Today as we walk back from the well, Teresita tells the children how she and I met Fidel and got to be photographed with him.

"Weren't you scared to meet El Comandante?" Pepo asks.

"It was a little scary," I reply. "Especially when he looks straight at you. It seems he can see right through you!"

"I can't believe you met him in person," Pepino remarks.

"I think I would faint if I got near him," Pepa says with a shiver.

"I stood as close to him as I am close to all of you now," I say.

"We could have touched his beard, if we'd wanted to, except he's so tall neither of us could reach it!" Teresita adds.

We all laugh and keep strolling, and soon the children run ahead of us. Then we hear them excitedly calling to us.

"¡Mira, mira, mira! Come quick, Teresita and Alegra, vengan!"

We set down our buckets and rush over.

And we see it, at last, the zunzuncito! The little hummingbird that only lives in Cuba, of all the places where it could live in the whole wide world.

I can't believe how precious the teeny-tiny bird is. How it sparkles and catches the light. How fast it flutters its wings as it hovers in the air. It's such a wonder of nature, and we are all giddy with joy at the sight of it!

46

An Alarming Letter

Later, after the joy of seeing the zunzuncito, an alarming letter arrives from Mamá that I read over and over, not knowing what to do, what to expect.

July 5, 1961

Mi querida hijica Alegra,
Your letter took a long time to arrive, but I was so glad to finally receive news from you. I was worried about how you might be managing in the countryside and was glad to hear you are getting enough to eat, and the people you are with treat you well. Our neighbor Carlos told us that you and Teresita were sent to Melena del Sur, so at least I knew where you were.

I didn't want your father to read your letter because he is still unhappy you are working for the revolution. I hid it, but then he kept asking if you'd written and I had to show it to him so he'd stop worrying. He didn't react too badly. But then he saw the picture in the newspaper of you smiling next to Fidel Castro! That made him furious! He says you've been brainwashed and is threatening to go to Melena del Sur and bring you home. I don't know how he'll do that, as we have no money, and if he makes a scene taking you away from the literacy brigade, he knows he'd get in trouble with the government. But if he does arrive in Melena del Sur, please treat him kindly but do what you think is best. I can only imagine how special this time is for you.

Now I must tell you our news. Your older brothers and sister and your nephews left Cuba suddenly, just yesterday. It feels very odd for your father and me to have none of our children nearby, and we are feeling quite heartbroken. I will explain more when I see you.

For now, know that your father and I miss you terribly, but I am grateful you are getting to have this experience.

Tu Mamá ke te kere muncho

47

A Handful of Mangos

The day after Mamá's letter reaches me, Papá arrives. His cousin, Rubén, borrowed a broken-down jalopy. They left when it was still dark out to get to Melena by morning.

The car screeches to a halt, and the sound is so frightening we all rush outside to see what has happened.

Papá doesn't scream. He simply says, "Alegra, get your things. We must go."

"But why, Papá?" I ask. "I want to stay. The people are good here, and I'm teaching them to read and write."

"Hijica, please. I really need you at home." I have never seen Papá cry and am shocked to see him wipe away a tear.

He looks older than old, his brow more wrinkled than when I said goodbye to him on Calle Obispo. The fury that used to drive him seems to have turned into the saddest sadness. I'm not sure which is worse.

But now I can't say no to him.

Gloria stands at the door. "What is it, niña? What has happened? Who is that man?"

"That's my father. I'm sorry, Gloria. Something's come up, and my family needs me. I have to go."

I step inside and quickly gather my things, leaving behind the hammock, the lantern, and the books and pencils I was given at the training camp.

I hug Gloria goodbye.

"Be well, niña, you taught us so much in so little time," she says. And Alfredo squeezes my shoulder, and I feel the knot of his mangled right hand.

It pains me the most to say goodbye to Teresita, and to have to leave her. We were supposed to be maestras together, and help and support each other throughout the literacy campaign.

"I'm sorry, Teresita, lo siento mucho," I tell her. "These have been the happiest days of my life. I'm so glad we finally became friends!"

"Don't be sorry, Alegra. I understand. I will miss you, but everything will be all right. I'll take over for you and be sure that Gloria and Alfredo continue to study and write their thank-you letter to Fidel."

It's so kind of Teresita to try to put my mind at rest, and it helps me feel less devastated.

Then I say goodbye to Ramona and Francisco, and Pepo, Pepino, and Pepa come to hug me. "I'm going to miss you all," I tell them. "I'll remember forever that you three showed me a zunzuncito! Promise me you'll keep looking until you find another one."

They nod their heads in unison, and when Pepa says, "Don't worry, we'll take care of Teresita; we already love her like a sister," I have to hold back my tears.

Gloria steps away, and I imagine it's because she doesn't want to see me leave, but she goes to her yard and returns with a handful of mangos.

"They will ripen in a few days. Take them home with you. So you won't forget us."

"I will never forget you," I say, and cry all the way back to Havana.

48

It Is Time for You to Sing Again

I'm grateful Papá doesn't say much on the trip back from Melena del Sur, just turns around from the front seat every now and then as if to reassure himself I am still there. When we arrive at Calle Oficios, I look up and see Mamá on the balcony. She waves her handkerchief to me as she did when I left.

Papá says to go upstairs; he'll be back later.

"Hijica, you decided to return," Mamá says as I come in the door. "It was your choice."

"Yes, Mamá, no one forced me. It was the tears in Papá's eyes that brought me home."

"You are a good daughter, dear Alegra. Your papá had decided not to get you, but after your brothers and sister left so hastily, he realized we must be together. We don't know what is going to happen here from day to day."

We embrace for a long time to make up for the months I've been away.

"And those mangos?" she asks.

"They're a gift from a señora named Gloria, in whose

house I was living, with her husband, Alfredo. They're kind people. I was sorry to leave them . . ."

"It will be nice to have something sweet to eat after all the bitterness."

"So tell me, Mamá. What has happened?"

"Well, after you joined the literacy campaign, things got worse here, and more and more people we know began to pack their suitcases to leave Cuba. When León, Flora, and José heard there was a plane going to Israel and that Jews didn't need passports or papers, they decided to flee. Practically overnight they were all gone. Just like that, poof, on a plane, up in the air!"

"Oh, Mamá, how terrible for you."

"Yes, truly terrible! We would have left too if you had been here. So now your father is trying to see if there is another flight for us."

"So what happened with León and Flora and José?"

"You remember León telling us how the shoe store where he worked was going to be taken away from the owner? Well, León lost his job, so he went to work at a bank and couldn't bear to see people being forced to convert all their money to a new worthless currency. And Flora and her husband were horrified when their boys kept playing a game where they pretended to be rebels spying to see if their parents were saying bad things about the revolution. And José was getting frustrated with his job at the pharmacy. There's no longer enough medicine to go around. When he refused to accept the bribes of the militiamen who wanted medicine for their families, they beat him up and called him a worthless turco and said next time they saw him it would be worse."

"Oh no, that's awful! And what about Papá?"

"Then your papá got into trouble. He'd been warned to stop peddling, but you know how stubborn he is. When he made a sale the other day, he was thrilled. Maybe he was smiling too much after that, because two militiamen stopped him on Calle Amargura and reminded him that peddling was against the law—there was no more private business in Cuba. Everyone must be working for the good of the revolution."

"And what did Papá do?"

"Your father, instead of apologizing, said to them that he was not going to work for anyone but himself. The milicianos beat him and stole his money and the shirts. He spent two weeks in jail. If not for his cousin, Rubén, who has ties with the government, he might have rotted away in there. Now he's free, but he's on their list, so any day they could find another reason to arrest him . . . That's what's happened."

"I had no idea, Mamá."

"How could you know? We have nothing, hijica. Nothing. We're living on handouts from the synagogue until we can figure out a way to leave. But if you want to stay . . ."

"Mamá, how could you even think I'd stay here without you and Papá?"

"But you love being a brigadista . . ."

"I do! I did! I'm proud I got to be a brigadista. Fidel says those who don't love the revolution are worms and don't love Cuba. He's wrong! I love Cuba, and still I'll leave my country to be with you and Papá, even if I'll be called a gusana."

Papá returns home late at night. He tells us, "The only one who can leave right away is you, Alegra. There are no planes going to Israel anymore, so we'll go to the United States. Children can leave without papers. We will have to come later once we have our papers."

"I'm going to travel all by myself?"

"Don't worry, hijica. You just have to get on the plane, and it's a short flight to Miami. There's an organization called HIAS. It stands for the Hebrew Immigrant Aid Society. They're a group who help Jews that need to leave their home and start a new life somewhere else. They'll be waiting for you at the airport in Miami."

"When do I leave?"

"Tomorrow," he replies. "You'll be on a plane with lots of other young people leaving Cuba without their parents."

"And when will you and Mamá come?"

"As soon as we can. It might take a little while."

"Then, Mamá, you must sing a song for me on the oud."

"May I, Moshico?" she asks Papá.

Both of them have tears in their eyes.

He nods. "Yes, Reina, please sing. It is time for you to sing again."

Papá takes the oud down from its hook on the wall and says, "Let's not hang it up there anymore. Keep it here, on the chair, so you can sing when you want." Then he embraces her gently, and she begins:

En la mar hay una torre...
In the sea there is a tower...

49

We Will Be Together Soon

In the morning, I stand on the balcony and look out at the sea one last time. When I come back inside I see Gloria's still-green mangos on the table. I feel sad I won't be around to taste them.

As I finish packing my suitcase, Mamá sews the necklace with the Star of David into the hem of the dress I will wear on the trip.

"Why are you doing that, Mamá? Can't I just wear it under my dress?"

"No jewelry can be taken out of Cuba. If they spot you wearing it at the airport, they'll take it away. Once you're in Miami, open the seam, but be careful, Alegra, that you don't tear the fabric."

"I'll be careful, Mamá, I promise."

Mamá looks at me with tears in her eyes. "I can't believe I have to send you away by yourself. I'm so sorry."

"It's not your fault, Mamá, and we will be together soon. And you're not sending me away. I'm choosing to go."

"Yes, yes, you are right, my daughter. How did you get to be the wise one?" she says with a smile.

Papá went out early, before I awoke. He returns drenched in sweat and hands me a pocket-size Spanish-English dictionary. "This is for you, hijica, something useful, I hope. I traded it for two shirts. No one has money anymore."

"Gracias, Papá," I say, touched by his unexpected gift.

I look at them both, my father and my mother, and have never felt closer to them than at this time of parting. I don't want to imagine that tomorrow we will no longer be together.

At the airport, there is one last area where we can wave goodbye before we part ways. A glass wall separates me from Papá and Mamá. He nods stiffly and turns away to hide his tears, but Mamá brings her face to the glass, to try to kiss me through that barrier, and I want to do the same but I can't— I'm too embarrassed.

Before I board the plane, an immigration officer peers inside my suitcase. He finds the dictionary and pulls it out.

"This stays here. We're running out of them. Too many of you are leaving for Miami."

"Please, it was a gift from my papá."

"Go, niña. Or do you want me to keep rummaging through your things?" He gazes at my neck and hands.

"You're not wearing jewelry, are you? You can't take that out of the country."

"No, compañero, I'm not wearing jewelry," I reply. And I rush off, not looking back, sad to have lost Papá's gift but grateful I still have the necklace.

And then I'm on the plane. I have no idea where I'm going and if anyone will really be there to take care of me on the other side of the sea. Dozens of other kids surround me. None of us dare say a word. We sit waiting for someone to breathe life into us. Only some very young ones, four or five years old, cry desperately and keep repeating, "Mami, where are you? Mami, where are you?"

As we rise into the air, everything below looks so small. I try to think of the future—to look forward to the places I'll go, the people I'll meet.

I remember how happy Teresita and I were when we rode the bus to the literacy campaign and our journey as brigadistas was just beginning. All we wanted was to do something good for people in Cuba. And we did!

Seeing Gloria write her name for the first time, seeing Alfredo read his name for the first time, how incredible to have witnessed them becoming literate. I'm not sure if there's anything more beautiful than teaching others to read and write. Maybe, somehow, someday, I will be able to continue performing this miracle.

CHAPTER 50

Please Don't Make Me an Orphan

Miami, August 6, 1961

Dear Mamá and Papá,
I hope you are well. It's been three weeks with no news of you, and I'm worried and wondering why you're delayed. I wish you had a telephone, even to hear your voices for a moment, but a letter will also make me happy. Please write as soon as you can!

So let me tell you how things have been for me. At first there wasn't anywhere for most of the kids on the plane to go, so we were placed in a Catholic orphanage. I didn't know until then that we were part of an exodus of thousands of children sent here by parents who don't want us growing up in communist Cuba. They call us Pedro Pan children because we've been sent to live in Neverland while we wait for our parents to come and find us.

I'll tell you the truth—the orphanage was horrible,

and I had to sleep on the top of a triple-decker bunk bed that was so high, I was squished against the ceiling. At night it was hard to sleep with all the crying children.

I am much happier now to be living with foster parents. They are nice people. He is a doctor, and the wife is often in pain because she suffers from kidney stones. HIAS placed me with them since they are Jewish, but they know nothing about Cuba or Sephardic traditions, and treat me like a country bumpkin that washed up on the shores of their house in Miami Beach. "Did you wear shoes in Cuba?" they ask me. I try to explain to them in my broken English that I was a volunteer in the literacy campaign, and thousands of brigadistas, many of them girls like me, were working to make Cuba an island of literate and educated people. But they look at me puzzled and say, "Really, darling? Your parents let you go all by yourself to the jungle? My oh my."

I am learning a lot of interesting American customs. The people here are always in a rush, and I find it funny that they politely say "excuse me, excuse me," as they push you out of the way in a crowded bus or store.

My foster parents think I was starving in Cuba, and so they like to take me to this restaurant called Wolfie's, where we eat enormous pastrami sandwiches and bowls of matzoh ball soup. It's all good, but, Mamá, I miss your borekas and bulemas, and your honey-filled baklava.

I miss you so much, and all I have to remember you now is a photo of you in my wallet. Papá, you're wear-

ing a white shirt and tie, and, Mamá, you're wearing a flowered dress. You both stare right into the camera. To me it seems you're looking straight into my heart. I am waiting eagerly for you both to be here, for you, Mamá, to sing and play the oud, and for you, Papá, to find friends with whom to play dominoes. Please send me a few words. Let me know you are well. Tell me you are coming soon. Please don't make me an orphan!

With all my love,
your hijica Alegra

PS: The other letter in the envelope is for Teresita. Please give it to her parents to pass along to her. I want her to know I haven't forgotten her.

PART FOUR

Paloma
2003

51

So Much Had to Happen Before I Could Be Born

"There are going to be thousands of people in this heat, including me," my dad declares as he packs water and granola bars in his knapsack. "I have to go and say goodbye to Celia Cruz. She was our queen of salsa. One of her last wishes was that she be brought to Miami so Cubans here could bid her farewell before her funeral in New York."

My mom gets teary-eyed. She's still in pajamas and sipping her morning coffee. "We danced to her music at our wedding, Rolando. She was such a part of our lives. I'd like to go, but you know how I hate big crowds. Will you say goodbye for both of us?"

"I understand, mi amor, of course."

Suddenly I hear myself saying, "Wait, Papi, I want to go!"

"You do, Paloma? We'll have to walk a lot. You're sure?"

"I'm sure."

"Okay, then let's go, mi niña."

We drive as close as we can to Biscayne Boulevard and park the car. It's a long trek, and keeping up with my dad isn't easy. He's got long legs and he walks fast.

I'm sweaty and out of breath by the time we get close to the Freedom Tower, which is draped in a Cuban flag. The crowd spills every which way, and the line to see Celia Cruz lying in state seems to go on forever.

"You know what the Freedom Tower represents, Paloma?"

"Yes, Papi, I know. Abuela told me. That's where Cubans went when they first arrived in Miami to get their documents and be allowed into the country as refugees."

"That's right. For many, it was the first stop on the road to freedom."

We take our place in line, among people singing along with the song on the loudspeaker about how life is a carnival—*la vida es un carnaval*—and we should spend more time singing than crying.

But lots of people *are* crying as they remember Celia. Many are waving Cuban flags, and others are holding up pictures of Celia flashing her beautiful smile. Someone shouts, "¡Azúcar!" as Celia did at the end of every song, and the crowd responds, "¡Azúcar!"

"Papi, why did Celia always say 'azúcar'? Was it because Cuba produces sugar?"

"Yes, sugar is the sweetness that comes from Cuba, but she also wanted to remind us of the bitterness felt by Afro-Cubans who were enslaved on the sugarcane plantations."

"Like our own ancestors."

"Like our own ancestors, that is true. How they suffered, and yet they held on to so many African traditions and music. Like our Celia."

We stand in line for hours in the July heat, but I don't mind. The line keeps moving, Celia's music keeps playing, and Papi tells me stories I've never heard before.

"Did you know when I was growing up in Cuba, you could go to jail for owning a Celia Cruz album? That's because she spoke out against Fidel Castro. And so he never let her return to Cuba, not even for her own mother's funeral."

"Did you get into trouble for having a Celia Cruz album?"

"I sure did, Paloma. I also got into trouble for having an Afro and playing Afro-Cuban music. Oh, and for wearing bell-bottoms. Can you believe it? They sent me to a work camp. To rehabilitate me, as they called it. After that, I knew I had to leave, and so I did when they opened the port of Mariel to any Cubans who wanted to go. I left on a boat that almost sank."

"Wow, Papi, I didn't know all this. I'm sure glad you made it here and married Mami!"

"I'm sure glad about that too." He smiles as he squeezes my shoulder. "Come on! Looks like we're next."

At last we move into the Freedom Tower and stand

before the coffin of Celia Cruz. Now a sad song is playing over the loudspeaker. The mournful notes remind me of the old Spanish songs I'm learning from my abuela.

"Papi, what's this song?"

"It's called 'Por si acaso no regreso,' and it's about Celia realizing she might never be able to see Cuba again. It's the way many of us Cubans feel. I don't know if I'll ever return either. After the pain I went through there, it hurts to think of going back, even though I miss my family."

I've never seen Papi cry. Now I see him wipe away tears.

My tears come too. But I also feel swept away by the power of music—and I'm proud that an Afro-Cuban woman who sang in Spanish could move the hearts of so many.

My dream to be a singer feels real here, and I think about my roots. I'm Afro-Cuban on my dad's side and Sephardic-Cuban on my mom's. My parents met briefly in Cuba when they were my age and he was playing the batá drums at her friend Teresita's house. Years later they ran into each other again at a drum circle in Miami Beach and fell in love, and that's how I came into the world.

As we drive home, passing the sleek buildings facing the sea on Collins Avenue, I am reminded of our upcoming trip to Spain. "Papi, I just realized that if Celia had died next week, we wouldn't have been able to pay our respects. We'd be away."

"That's right, Paloma. Perhaps the stars aligned so we could be here. It was meant to be—kismet, as your abuela likes to say. And I'm sure it's meant to be that we're going to Spain."

"Really, Papi? What do you mean?"

"Well, we say we're taking a vacation, but you know this trip's going to be much more than that for your abuela and your mami. It's going to be emotional. Maybe for you too. You have ancestors who were forced out of Spain. They were refugees long before that word existed."

My dad's words echo inside me. I feel like I carry a lot of history on my shoulders. Not only were my ancestors driven out of Spain, but my abuela had to leave Turkey, and my parents had to leave Cuba. So many seas were crossed. So much had to happen before I could be born here in this place.

I make a promise to myself that I will write a song about their journeys and will sing it in Spanish, like Celia, when I grow up.

52

Keeper of Memories

Mangos always remind my mom of her girlhood in Cuba. Every time she bites into one, she starts to reminisce. "It was the most beautiful thing, living in the countryside among the mango trees," she says now as the juice dribbles down her chin. "Oh, and seeing the zunzuncito—the tiniest hummingbird in the world. It only exists in Cuba!"

The two of us sit on our seventh-floor balcony, gazing at the sea, taking in the afternoon breeze. Papi will be home late. He's got to catch up on work at the television station, where he's a sound technician, before our trip to Spain.

My mom's life seems incredible to me, and I love hearing her relive every detail of the days when she and Teresita, my dad's cousin, were brigadistas in the literacy campaign in Cuba—an experience that inspired her to become a literacy specialist and teach children, as well as farmworkers, to read and write. She has piles of thank-you cards from her grateful students. And lots of letters from Teresita, which take forever to get here from Cuba.

I can't believe she was only twelve—the same age as I am now—when she left home to be a brigadista and then had to leave Cuba by herself as a refugee. And she never saw her father again.

While my mom continues to reminisce, I reach for my guitar and strum a few notes in a minor key that have a melancholy edge to them.

She raises an eyebrow. "Where did you learn to play the guitar like that?"

"Abuela's been teaching me some old songs. She sings and I strum along."

My mom bites into another mango and then says, "Did she tell you about her oud?"

"Her what?"

"The oud. I guess she didn't tell you."

"What's an oud?"

"It's a stringed instrument, kind of like a lute. She brought it with her from Turkey to Cuba when she was a girl. But it got left behind in Cuba—the officials at the airport wouldn't let her take it out of the country, and she was heartbroken. It was a gift from her mother."

"That's awful. I'd be so sad if anything ever happened to the necklace you gave me."

I hold up the necklace with the Jewish star and see it gleam as it catches a ray of sunlight.

My mom sighs. "It wasn't easy to get that necklace out of Cuba."

"I know, Mami. You've told me the story. Abuela sewed it into the hem of your dress, and that's how you got it out of the country. But they took away the dictionary your father gave you."

"You remember everything, Paloma! You're a keeper of memories, aren't you?"

"I guess I am. That's why I'm so excited we're going to Spain! It's amazing to think I'll be in the land of our ancestors. Maybe some buried memories will come back."

My mom wipes away the mango juice from her chin and looks at me quizzically, or is it pityingly? "Don't get your hopes up, Paloma. Five hundred years is a *long* time, and if our family was forced to leave during the Spanish Inquisition, some of the memories could be bitter."

"But that's the point. Even with all the suffering our families went through, we survived. We're here to tell the story."

"You're right, sweetheart. I like how you look on the bright side. Now please, play some happy songs too. Your abuela's songs are so weepy."

"That's easy," I say. "Here's a song you love."

I strum my guitar and sing Celia Cruz's "La vida es un carnaval," and my mom joins in. Together, at the top of our lungs, we sing about how you have to live singing—hay que vivir cantando. No one is around on the neighboring balconies, so we sing to the sea, watching the sky turn pink.

As the day fades away, I press the Jewish star on the necklace against my skin and feel its imprint. I am filled with a light from deep inside, knowing that my mom wore it when she was my age, and before that my grandmother wore it too.

53

You Must Learn the Song and Remember It by Heart

I feel so lucky Abuela lives in the same building as we do. It's easy to visit her—as long as you call in advance.

"I'm not a little viejita who sits at home waiting for people to look in on her," she says, and it's true. She likes to keep busy and is often out at her favorite markets or restaurants, where everyone knows her name is Reina, or she's home entertaining her lady friends, serving up lemony stuffed grape leaves, feta-filled spinach pie, thin slices of breaded eggplant, and her famous baklava swimming in honey.

Now I sit with her in her sunny living room and slip my guitar out of its case. "I hear you used to play an instrument called the oud," I say.

"Yes, I loved it. I wish I had it still so you could play it," she tells me. "To this day I can't believe they wouldn't let me bring it when I left Cuba. We were allowed one suitcase, and that was it."

"Mami said she only had one suitcase too. It must have been hard for you to let her leave Cuba by herself."

My grandmother shudders at the memory. "So hard!

I thought we'd only be separated for a few weeks at most. Your grandfather was in trouble with the government, and we imagined they'd be eager to rid themselves of a troublemaker. Instead they jailed him, and we were stuck there. When they finally released him, he was very sick. He died soon after. So I packed up my clothes, a photo album, and the keys to my apartment in Cuba and to my childhood house in Turkey."

Abuela pulls out her key chain. "See? Here's the key to this apartment. And here are the ones to the homes I lost. The homes I'll never see again. I carry them all. Not to forget."

I touch the old keys. They're rusty and feel heavier than the new key, as if carrying the weight of more memories.

"What was it like when you saw Mami again after being separated for so long?"

Abuela takes a deep breath and says, "My Alegra, the joy of my life, was twelve when she left Cuba. When I saw her again in Miami, she was fifteen. I was sad I missed three years of her life, and she was angry I had been absent. It took a while, but we became close again."

"And you supported her when she wanted to marry Papi?"

"Yes! Our Cuban Sephardic community was surprised that she chose to marry outside our faith—and to an Afro-Cuban—but I said she should marry who she loved. Then your papi outsmarted the community and converted to Judaism. So they had to accept him."

"That's my papi!" I say, feeling so proud of him.

I begin strumming the melancholy tune on my guitar, and after a while, I say, "Teach me more of that song you sang for me the other day."

And Abuela begins to sing along:

En la mar hay una torre,
en la torre una ventana,
en la ventana una hija
que a los marineros llama.

In the sea there is a tower,
in the tower there is a window,
at the window a daughter
who calls to the sailors.

She sings it several more times, making sure I know each word and pronounce it properly in Ladino—the old Judeo-Spanish her ancestors spoke.

Hija, I learn, is said as "ee-sha" instead of "ee-ha" as in Spanish. It's difficult to learn it all, but Abuela is patient with me.

I finally have the melody down and can accompany her pretty well.

"Abuela, they say Ladino is an endangered language, so thank you for teaching me."

"It's funny—I didn't know it was called Ladino when I spoke it with my family in Turkey. We thought we were speaking Spanish, mixed with a few words of Italian, Turkish, French, Hebrew, and Arabic, the languages from the places where our people dwelled after they left Spain. It was Spanish from five hundred years ago because we never returned after we were expelled."

"Do you know where we come from, Abuela? What part of Spain?"

"Mima, my beautiful mother, your great-grandmother, used to say we came from Toledo. Her last name was Toledano, after all."

"Right! And now we're going to Spain, so we'll have to visit Toledo!"

Abuela brings her hand to her heart. "I'm getting palpitations just thinking about it!"

"Oh no, Abuela, are you okay?"

"Don't worry, mi Paloma." She laughs. "It's not serious. It's the excitement! Who would have thought at ninety-one I'd be setting foot for the first time in the land of our ancestors. Mashallah, mashallah."

"Abuela, you say that a lot—mashallah."

"Yes. It's an Arabic word that means 'with God's blessing.' We said it all the time in Turkey, as we had many Muslim neighbors. We learned a lot of their beliefs and traditions."

"I know, Abuela. Like the way you're always trying to ward off the evil eye."

"That's right, mi Paloma. You haven't lost that lucky eye pin I gave you?"

"Of course not, Abuela. You never know when you'll need it."

We laugh and hug each other. Then I strum a few notes on the guitar and realize I've forgotten some of the words of the song that Abuela taught me.

"Can I have pen and paper to write down the words of the song?"

"No, mi Paloma, you must learn the song and remember it by heart. Then no one can ever take it away from you."

I play the song about the girl trapped in the tower again, and Abuela gets a faraway look in her eyes.

"Are you okay, Abuela?"

"Hearing the song now brought back the memory of a good friend from Turkey. His name was Sadik . . . I'll never know what became of him." And suddenly she's wiping away tears.

"I'm sorry, Abuela. Do you think we're being too melancholy? Mami says she doesn't want me to be sad. She says I shouldn't steep myself in so much history and all these weepy Sephardic songs. But what is it that draws you and me to such mournful music?"

"I think it fills our souls," Abuela says. "We all have a piece of ourselves that's lost and we will never get back. Those sad songs remind us that we are all searching for something that perhaps we will never find . . ."

54

A Tale Across Five Hundred Years

I'm in the window seat, watching as we take off, the plane rising above the bright lights of Miami. Abuela sits next to me, and my mom and dad are in the row in front of us.

Within minutes, we leave behind the firmness of land, and we're flying over the sea.

"Look, Abuela! How much sea there is!"

Abuela draws closer and looks out. "Yes, so much sea," she says. "But it isn't as overpowering on a plane as it is on a ship. I'm glad we're far above and can't hear the roar of the waves!"

She opens her large handbag, and immediately there's a familiar scent of home. Abuela has packed a few of her delicious potato-and-cheese borekas, each wrapped in aluminum foil, and she pulls them out and passes them around to my mom and my dad and then to the two of us.

"Have them now, while they're still a little warm," she says, as if we're having a picnic on the beach instead of crossing the sea to go to Spain.

Soon after we've eaten, she dozes off, and my mom and dad settle in to watching movies.

I've brought a travel book about Spain to read on the plane and turn to the chapter about Toledo. The first thing I learn is that it was known as the city of three cultures, and that Jews, Muslims, and Christians lived together peacefully for centuries.

Today, one of the biggest tourist attractions is its medieval Jewish neighborhood, which looks like a storybook village in the photographs, with its stone buildings and winding alleys. But the Jewish population was destroyed during the Spanish Inquisition. And they actually burned people at the stake if they appeared to be holding on to Jewish traditions. So while it might look like a storybook village, awful things happened there.

As I read about all this, I realize I'm part of a tale across five hundred years. It's a tale that might seem fascinating to a tourist, but it's making me feel like a dove with broken wings.

I hope, hope, hope my ancestors didn't suffer.

I remind myself I have nothing to fear. I'm not alone, and the Inquisition ended a long time ago.

And then I remember Abuela's gift. As she sleeps by my side, I pull out of my pocket the lucky eye charm she gave me and pin it inside my T-shirt.

55

Maybe Lorca's Ghost Has Met the Ghosts of My Ancestors

The hotel where we're staying in Madrid overlooks the Plaza de Santa Ana, and our rooms are side by side, one for my parents, one for me and Abuela. The balconies open onto the street, and you can hear the laughter of people at all hours. In the morning, the delivery workers wheel the goods to stores and restaurants and cafés. The churrería on the corner fills the air with the scent of hot chocolate and sugary dough.

While my dad goes off to a work meeting, Mami, Abuela, and I stroll around the neighborhood. It's boiling hot in late July, so we move at a turtle's pace so as to not tire Abuela. Now and then, Abuela takes my hand and says, "We are in Spain! Estamos en La Espanya!"

When we're ready to rest, we have tapas at one of the cafés on the Plaza de Santa Ana, next to a statue of the poet and playwright Federico García Lorca. He's holding a nightingale between his hands, and it's about to fly into the sky.

My mom tells us she studied the poems of Lorca when she

was in college. She recites one from memory about a great matador who was killed at five o'clock in the afternoon.

A las cinco de la tarde.
Eran las cinco en punto de la tarde . . .

She pauses and looks at her watch. "How do you like that? It's five o'clock on the dot right now." She lets out a sigh. "I love it when literature and life collide. Some of the last words of the poem are coming back to me too. I remember it goes like this—"

No te conoce nadie. No. Pero yo te canto.
No one knows you. No. But I sing of you.

Our waiter overhears my mom's impromptu poetry recital and tells us that the statue was built years ago and kept in storage for over a decade because Spaniards are divided in their feelings for Lorca. Some think he was a hero, executed during the Spanish Civil War because he was gay and a socialist, while others think he was a traitor who deserved his cruel death.

"His remains have never been found," the waiter adds in a whisper. "It's said Lorca's ghost still wanders around Spain looking for a place to rest."

Abuela replies, "Maybe Lorca's ghost has met the ghosts of my ancestors."

"Who are your ancestors, señora, if I may ask?" the

waiter says politely. "You speak Spanish very well, but with an accent I can't quite place."

"My ancestors were sefarditas," Abuela replies. "Sephardic Jews who lived here long, long ago. We think some left during the Inquisition so they could continue being Jewish, and others converted and became Catholics to stay here in the land they loved. My Spanish is the old language of Spain mixed with other languages from our many homes. Nowadays we call it Ladino. We used to call it simply espanyol. The three of us here, we each speak a different kind of Spanish. I was born in Turkey and my daughter in Cuba and my granddaughter in Miami."

"I see, I see," the waiter replies, stroking his chin. "I am glad you have returned to the land that was once your home. Let me offer you a little something on the house. We call it mosto; it is the juice of the grapes, nice and sweet, with no alcohol, so it is fine for the young girl to drink as well."

"Gracias," Abuela and my mom say. "Agradecida," I add, speaking my best, most formal Spanish.

"¡Qué bueno que todas hablan español!" the waiter responds merrily, and comes back with three long-stemmed wineglasses filled with mosto, which is so delicious I plan to drink it every day I'm in Spain!

On our way back to the hotel, I stop and look up at the statue of Lorca. I imagine his hands opening and the nightingale arising and spreading its wings.

56

We'll Be Surrounded by History There

The balcony in my parents' room is open, letting in the glimmer of a Madrid sunset. We're snacking on olives, bread, and cheese as we prepare for our trip to Toledo tomorrow.

Abuela's eyes have her faraway look. "Mima always said our family was from Toledo, because our last name was Toledano. Who knows if it's true?"

"Tomorrow when we visit, we may find out more," my mom says. "It's so exciting to be going there."

My dad nods. "And I have a surprise. I've arranged for a private visit at the Sinagoga del Tránsito, which dates from before 1492. It's been restored and is now the Museo Sefardí."

"That's great, Papi! And what hotel are we staying at? Is it in the neighborhood where the Jewish people once lived?" I ask.

"Yes! Our hotel is right in the heart of the judería. That's what they call the old Jewish neighborhood. You know what they told me? 'You'll be surrounded by history there.'

They said we're going to feel like we've been transported to another time."

"Well, I hope not back to the Inquisition!" Abuela says.

"No, no," I say, and take her hand. "To *before* that. When Toledo was a welcoming place for all kinds of different people to live."

Abuela hugs me. "Gracias, mi Paloma, you are a wise one. And the light of my life."

"Mine too," my mom agrees.

And my dad adds, "Yes. You and your generation give us hope for a better future, Paloma."

"All right. Let's not give too many compliments now," Abuela says. "We adore Paloma, but we don't want to give her the evil eye!" She brings her hands to my head and recites the blessing, "Paths of milk and honey, kaminos de leche i miel, good paths only for you, dearest nieta. May our Dio guard you from all evil."

"Gracias, Abuela. And is it okay to say amen?"

"Of course, mi Paloma!"

And with that blessing—plus the Jewish star necklace *and* the lucky eye pin—I feel prepared for whatever awaits us in Toledo.

57

Are You Ready for the Tour?

At the crack of dawn we head to Toledo. My dad has rented a car, and we drive across the dry terrain of red earth and hardy olive trees. Heading farther and farther into a countryside without even a hint of sea, I realize I have spent my whole life looking out at it. I don't know if I could ever live far from the sea.

I sit with Abuela in the back seat, the two of us looking out the window. My mom is in the front seat next to my dad, and every few minutes she turns around to gaze at us, as if making sure we're still there. "Todo bien, hijica," Abuela says consolingly each time she looks back.

At last, the city appears on the horizon. "Look, there it is!" I exclaim.

Toledo sits on top of a hill, surrounded by the Río Tajo—the Tagus River. We enter through one of the ancient walled gates into the old city, driving slowly through the bumpy cobblestoned streets and narrow alleys. We seem to keep going in circles and have to ask for directions from tourists who are just as lost as we are.

Abuela brings her hand to her heart. "I don't like being lost."

"Hold my hand, Abuela," I say.

She clasps my hand tightly, as if she might float away otherwise.

My mom turns from the front seat and says to Abuela, "I understand how you're feeling, Mamá. It's strange to be here, where so much harm was done to our people."

"Come on, everything will be fine. We're just going to a museum," my dad says, and finally we reach the Sinagoga del Tránsito.

Inside, we meet Mari Luz, the person giving us a private tour. She's about my mom's age, with similar dark curly hair.

"Hola, buenos días," Mari Luz greets us. "So you are the familia cubana that's visiting Spain for the first time?"

"That's us!" my dad replies to her in Spanish. "But we don't live in Cuba anymore. Or I guess you could say we live in northern Cuba—also known as Miami."

Mari Luz laughs, then gives us all a kiss on each cheek. "It's wonderful you speak Spanish, since my English is not so good." She smiles at me. "You speak Spanish too?"

"You sort of can't live in Miami if you don't speak Spanish," I joke.

"You have your father's sense of humor! Tell me: What is your name? How old are you?"

"I'm Paloma. I'm twelve."

"Well, how do you like that? My daughter is also named

Paloma. We like to call her Palomita. She's a little younger than you, just turned ten."

"That's amazing," I say. "I don't know anyone else who shares my name."

"What a nice coincidence, really . . ." She smiles. "Well, are you ready for the tour?"

She leads us into the restored synagogue and points to a pew so Abuela can rest while she begins to explain its history.

"This synagogue was built in 1357. We believe the Jews of Toledo prayed here until their religion was outlawed in 1492. Then it became a church, then a military barrack, and now the Sephardic Museum. It's a place to remember the Jewish people who once lived here . . . and were forced out with so much cruelty."

Mari Luz takes a deep breath. I can tell this isn't just a canned speech for her.

I look up at the walls and ceiling, covered with elaborate designs and colorful etchings.

"The synagogue features a Mudéjar ceiling, a style of medieval Islamic architecture created by Muslims who lived in Spain," Mari Luz explains.

I point to the carved line of words that run along the top of the walls. "What are those inscriptions in Hebrew?"

"Good question, Paloma, muy bien." And she turns her gaze to the words at the center. "That line says, 'Of the graces of the Lord let us sing.'"

Abuela raises her arms into the air as if wanting to gather the experience and hold on to it. "This is beautiful. I can't believe my eyes . . . I could cry, it's so beautiful."

"It is a jewel," Mari Luz agrees. "So beautiful even a person who isn't religious might be inspired to recite a prayer here."

Afterward Mari Luz takes us to the museum. She tells us about the archaeological findings and how they're still digging around the synagogue and in the old town, looking for more clues about the Jews who once lived in Toledo.

"Have a look at this marble basin. See the menorah in the center? And there's a tree of life, a shofar, peacocks on either side, and an inscription in Hebrew asking for peace. It's from the time of the Romans. That means Jews were on this soil already long, long ago."

Then she takes us to a room exhibiting Jewish religious items. "That prayer shawl you see there was a donation from a Sephardic family whose ancestors were from Toledo," she tells us proudly. "And that Torah there, it's hundreds of years old and still intact. Just some of the writing has smudged. We think it's of Spanish origin. An antiques dealer discovered it in Istanbul and brought it to us."

As we follow along, she points to a large facsimile of the Edict of Expulsion hanging on the wall. "You can see the signatures of King Fernando and Queen Isabel, and the date, March 31, 1492. It's here so we won't forget the horror they unleashed with their words of intolerance and hate."

Soon Abuela tires from being on her feet, and my mom looks worn out too, so my dad takes his cue and says, "Mari Luz, gracias, this has been such a wonderful tour."

"But I must show you one more thing—a recent find just added to our collection."

She leads us to a small exhibition case with a glass cover that's in a corner of the room.

"The parchment you see here could be from the 1400s. It's Spanish written in Hebrew letters, and our scholars think it may have been written by a young person because of the calligraphy. So far, this is what we've been able to make out: *Adio mi Toledo, kerida caza, una vez fui Benvenida, agora no, a donde voy manyana es un misterio de nuestro Dio.*"

I translate it to myself as I hear it: *Goodbye, my Toledo, my beloved home, once I was welcome, now I am not, where I am going tomorrow is a mystery of our God.*

"That's sad," I say. "How horrible to be kicked out of your own home . . . Do you think a young girl could have written that?"

"Maybe," Mari Luz says. "Although there weren't many girls your age who could read and write at that time. But there were some who learned. Secretly."

"If she was a girl anything like you, mi Paloma, I'm sure she'd have insisted on knowing how to read and write," Abuela says.

"I agree. Let's claim this poet as our ancestor!" my mom chimes in. "What powerful words—*once I was benvenida, now I am not.*"

Hearing this, Mari Luz grows more animated. "The scholars find precisely that part of the text very interesting. The word *benvenida* is written in larger, darker letters than the rest of the text, so we think it might be the name of the poet. If so, then it could be a girl's name, Benvenida or Bienvenida, not simply the Spanish word for welcome. Maybe the poet was trying to tell us something."

"But how did the parchment survive for five hundred years?" I ask.

"It was well hidden in the stone wall of an ancient house here in Toledo," Mari Luz replies. "We think maybe it was placed there for safekeeping. We'll never know for sure, of course. The past is a lost country. You can only imagine it, like a dream."

58

If You Ever Hear from Reina Cohen Toledano

As Mari Luz leads us toward the museum's exit, we pass something in a large glass case that catches Abuela's eye.

"Look at that! An oud!" she exclaims as she gets closer. "And it looks so much like Mima's oud. The oud I carried from Turkey to Cuba!"

My mom stares into the case and gets excited too. "You're right, Mamá. It looks the same as your oud!"

"This oud was made in Turkey. It was a gift," Mari Luz tells us. "There's a bit of a personal story behind it, as it was a donation from my father-in-law. He was from Turkey."

"Well, I am Turkish," Abuela replies.

"Really? I thought you were Cuban," Mari Luz says, looking confused.

Abuela explains, "I should say, I was born in Turkey. I left for Cuba when I was twelve and never returned to Turkey, never saw my mother and father and my two sisters again."

Now it is Mari Luz who seems unsteady on her feet. "Don't tell me. I know this is very unlikely . . . but, by any chance, do you know a woman named Reina Cohen Toledano?"

"I am Reina Cohen Toledano," Abuela replies.

"What?" Mari Luz looks as if she's seen a ghost. She takes a breath and wipes her brow with a handkerchief. "This is too amazing! I have something to tell you. Come, let's sit down."

Mari Luz leads us to an empty seminar room and passes out drinks of water. After we've had a few sips, she says to Abuela, "My father-in-law, Sadik Topal, always said, 'If you ever hear from Reina Cohen Toledano, tell her I never forgot her.' I can say for sure, he never forgot you."

"Sadik from Silivri?" Abuela asks.

"Yes, Sadik from Silivri," Mari Luz repeats.

Now it's my grandmother's turn to look like she's seen a ghost. "Oh my, oh my, it can't be."

With tears in her eyes, Mari Luz continues. "My father-in-law told me the story many times. That your father sent you away to Cuba to marry because he thought you were too friendly with him. He remembered your singing and how beautifully you played the oud. So, after you left, he studied the oud and learned to sing Sephardic songs."

Abuela pulls out a handkerchief and dabs at her tears. "Sadik was the kindest friend. He was just my friend, we were only twelve, after all, but they couldn't understand such a friendship between a girl and a boy in those days. Because of that, we both suffered. But I can't believe he studied the oud and learned our songs."

Mari Luz nods. "He played the oud very well. Eventually, he went to Germany to study and brought the oud with him.

He became a biochemist. In Germany he met my mother-in-law. She was from Toledo and worked as a secretary at the university where he studied. After a few years, they decided to come here to live. That's how I met my husband, their son, who was born in Toledo, just like me."

I watch as Abuela listens, wiping away the last of her tears. I hope this isn't too much emotion for her. I know the question that must be on her mind, and I ask it for her.

"And Sadik, is he still alive?"

Mari Luz sighs sadly. "He died last year, after he turned ninety-one."

"What a pity, we missed him by a year," my mom says, and she too is teary-eyed.

Even my dad is wiping away tears.

So that I don't fall apart too, I blurt out, "Would it be all right if Abuela played the oud?"

"I think so. Let me take it out of the exhibition case. It hasn't been played in a while."

Mari Luz brings the oud to Abuela. Even with her arthritic fingers, Abuela strums the oud nimbly. Soon she is playing the song I've learned.

"Sing, Paloma, sing," Abuela requests, and I sing the words about the girl in the tower.

"Bello, bello," Mari Luz says when we're done, her eyes misted over. "And you won't believe it, but Sadik sang that song too."

"That song united us and separated us," Abuela replies wistfully.

"We're so lucky to have met you, Mari Luz," my mom says.

Abuela is quick to correct her statement. "Actually, it was a mix of good luck and what God willed that brought us together. Mashallah."

Mari Luz smiles. "Sadik always said 'mashallah' too."

59

A Lost Country

None of us feel ready to step out of the magic of the museum and into the world outside. At last my dad gently announces, "Well, we should be going. We still haven't checked into our hotel." He turns to Mari Luz. "We're staying at a place in the heart of the judería. They told us we'll feel like we've been transported to another time."

Mari Luz says she lives in the Jewish quarter and then surprises us with an invitation. "I'd be honored if you could join me and my husband Juan Carlos and our daughter Palomita this evening for Shabbat dinner."

"Shabbat dinner?" my mom asks, flabbergasted. "You celebrate Shabbat?"

"Yes, it's become our custom on Friday nights," Mari Luz replies. "Growing up in Toledo, I was convinced I came from a family of conversos. Our house is one of the oldest in the Jewish quarter. We didn't eat pork, and my grandmother never cooked on Saturdays. She also fasted once a year, right around this time, at the end of July, as if recalling the sorrow of the last days when the Jews left Spain."

My mom and dad happily accept the invitation, and Abuela looks mesmerized upon hearing all this. As we depart, she says softly, "Perhaps the past isn't such a lost country after all."

Our hotel is located in one of Toledo's narrow zigzagging alleys. After we park our car, I hold Abuela's arm as we inch down the alley. The cobblestones aren't easy on Abuela's feet, but I enjoy walking slowly and taking in the neighborhood.

All around are stores selling gold filigree jewelry and embroidered cloths in buildings where Jewish artisans must have labored centuries ago.

I'm enchanted by the ancient stone houses, still standing tall after the passage of so much time. I wish I could ask, *Stones, do you remember a girl named Benvenida?*

The air has a vaguely sweet scent I can't quite identify. I wish I could also ask, *Stones, has there always been this sweetness in the air? Even in the sad days of leaving Toledo?*

As Abuela and I freshen up to go to dinner, I think of her words about the ghosts of her Sephardic ancestors. Now I realize there are the ghosts of those who left and the ghosts of the conversos too. We were once one people, some choosing to hide, some choosing to flee. I clearly descend from the ones who fled, but I'm starting to think I may have had family who stayed.

And now I am walking on the path of those who came before me.

Whatever decisions were made by our ancestors, I imagine how joyous they'd be knowing we're alive now and finding one another.

60

The Scent of Almonds and Honey

"Come in, come in," Mari Luz says when we arrive. "Meet my husband, Juan Carlos."

"Buenas, buenas," Juan Carlos says, giving Abuela an extra-long hug.

"Selam," she says.

"Selam," Juan Carlos replies, also in Turkish.

"Forgive me for staring at you, but you resemble your father so closely I feel as if I'm seeing him again," Abuela marvels.

"I know! I am very turco, aren't I?" he replies, chuckling.

"You are, you are," Abuela says, and her face looks radiant.

When Palomita walks in with a book in her hand, her mother gazes at her proudly. "As you can see, our Palomita loves to read. She's always carrying a book around."

My mom practically leaps with joy as she greets Palomita. "I was part of a literacy campaign in Cuba when I was a girl. I think there's nothing more magnificent than books!"

Then I extend my hand to her, and say, "Paloma, yo soy Paloma también."

Hearing me say I too am Paloma, named after the dove of peace, makes her smile. She extends her hand back to me and then stays by my side and leans into me slightly, and it feels as if we've always known each other.

Mari Luz leads us to a table by the window, where two tall candles in silver candleholders are waiting to be lit.

"I light these every Friday night in memory of the Jewish people who once lived here. And I light them by the window so they can be seen," she tells us.

"Gracias," my dad says. "That's a beautiful thing to do."

After Mari Luz lights the candles and we say the Shabbat prayer together, we sit, and Juan Carlos tears us each a piece of braided challah bread. The meal is so good, and so familiar, with the eggplant prepared just like Abuela does it.

As we eat, I look around, and it feels like we've stepped into an alternate universe. Is this really happening?

Later, for dessert, Mari Luz brings out treats on a tray. They are shaped into half-moons and toasted on top. "Toledo is famous for this marzipan. It's made of almonds from the local trees and honey from the local hives. Its aroma has filled our streets for centuries."

And that's how I learn that the sweet scent in the air is the scent of marzipan.

When we've all finished, I break into a song by Flory Jagoda—a woman who was a champion of Sephardic music and sang in Ladino.

Buen Shabat, buen Shabat
kun salud i vida . . .

Good Shabbat, good Shabbat
with health and life . . .

"Bello, bello," Mari Luz says. "You sing so beautifully, Paloma. How did you learn?"

"Abuela is teaching me all the old Sephardic songs that she knows, and I'm also learning a few on my own."

Abuela, who is sitting across from me, reaches over and squeezes my hand. "We have fun singing together, don't we?"

"We do, Abuela, even when the songs are sad."

"Those are my favorites," Abuela says.

"I'd love to learn some," Palomita says.

"We'll be here a few days," I tell her. "I can teach you."

At this, Palomita lights up. "¡Qué bueno! And maybe I can show you around. I know lots of Toledo's history."

"That'd be great!" I say. "Every place here feels like it has a hidden story."

My mom nods. "I feel that too. Even though our ancestors were expelled hundreds of years ago, the houses and streets still seem filled with the memory of their presence."

My dad adds, "They told us at the hotel that they think part of their building was originally the home of a medieval Jewish family. What makes it unique is its large courtyard."

"That means you are staying where the parchment from

the museum was found. Found by our own Palomita," Mari Luz exclaims.

"It was an amazing discovery!" Palomita says. "I found it in one of the walls surrounding that courtyard."

Mari Luz smiles at her daughter. "Palomita is good at digging around and finding unexpected things. Perhaps she'll be an archaeologist someday."

"Oh, I would have so much fun spending my days looking for messages from the past and figuring out what they mean," Palomita says.

"Me too," I say. "I'm always curious about what the world was like before I was born. I'm known as the keeper of memories in our home."

"You are," my mom agrees. "You know my life story better than I do!"

"Looks like our girls share a passion for unraveling the mysteries of the past. Perhaps they'll uncover stories that aren't yet in the history books!" Mari Luz says. "How about tomorrow we stop by your hotel, Paloma, and Palomita can show you the exact spot in the wall where she found the hidden parchment?"

"Yes, please!"

I know I'll barely sleep waiting for tomorrow.

And then I say, "Gracias," and I realize I'm also saying thank you for all the blessings that brought me this far.

61

Toledo Won't Ever Forget You

Our room overlooks the hotel's courtyard, and tonight a sliver of the moon is shining down on it. Abuela is snoring gently, and I feel an urge to go outside. To stand in the place where Palomita found the ancient note.

I tiptoe into the courtyard in my nightgown. The warm air is sweet with the scent of marzipan and the roses that grow in the garden. From somewhere up above, a nightingale sings a beautiful song to me.

As I gaze at the enormous sky laced with jagged clouds and so many shining stars, I think of the ancestors who came before me.

When they gazed at these same stars, did they wish for some of the same things I do?

Freedom.

A home where we are welcome.

And where we can also welcome others.

I walk to the edge of the courtyard and touch the cool stone wall. I imagine the girl who lived here all those centuries ago. A girl who wrote those words on a parchment and decided to hide her message deep in one of the wall's crevices, hoping it might be found and mean something . . . to someone . . . like me.

And it does.

It reminds me I'm connected to those who came before me through the power of the words we speak, the words we write, the words we sing, the words in which we tell our dreams.

I wish I could go back five hundred years and whisper in her ear, "Toledo won't ever forget you." The most I can do is lift my voice, and to the night, the sky, the stars, and the moon, I say, "I'm here."

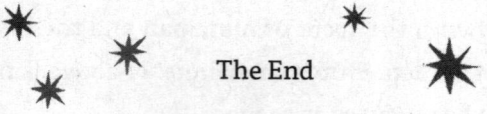

The End

Author's Note

I had two grandmothers I adored—Baba, my maternal grandmother, Esther, was a Polish Jew who became the inspiration for my book *Letters from Cuba*; and Abuela, my paternal grandmother, Rebeca, was a Turkish Jew. As young women, they sailed on different ships to Cuba in the 1920s to start a new life on the eve of the impending doom of the Holocaust. Baba brought with her the Yiddish language and the Ashkenazi culture of Eastern Europe. Abuela brought with her the language of Ladino, or Judeo-Spanish, and the culture of the Sephardic Jews, who trace their ancestry to Spain before the 1492 expulsion, the place they call Sefarad—which means Spain in Hebrew.

Baba, I knew very well, having spent countless hours with her, listening to her life story. Sadly, I barely knew Abuela, since I didn't grow up close to the paternal side of my family (though I was said to resemble the "turcos" more because of my dark hair and dark eyes).

But sometimes I think that even if I had been able to spend time with Abuela, I might not have learned much.

My family always said she didn't like to talk about herself. Abuela's life was mysterious. But I do know that she was warm and generous, and I loved that she called me Rutica and spoke a Spanish that sounded like poetry. She cooked delicious Sephardic food swimming in olive oil and desserts soaked in honey.

What the family knew about her life was that she'd been sent to Havana for an arranged marriage, but when she arrived, the man she was supposed to marry had married someone else. She had come alone, penniless, leaving behind her two sisters and a brother, and her parents, whom she never saw again. She brought an oud with her and liked to sing Sephardic songs. An uncle took her in, and she sat in the entranceway of his home in Luyanó in the afternoons, singing and playing the oud. The man who would become my abuelo heard her and fell in love. But after they married and had four children, she was too busy caring for her family. Her oud ended up hanging from a nail on the wall. My father says he never heard her play it, though the lady neighbors on Calle Oficios remembered she had played it beautifully in her youth. The oud was left behind when she fled from Cuba, a souvenir of a lost time in her life.

Inspired by these few details of Abuela's story, I sat down to write this novel, taking on a project I feared was going to be too difficult to pull off. I decided that to place Abuela's story in the larger context of Sephardic history, I would start in 1492. This was the year the Jews were expelled from Spain, following the end of Muslim rule in the Iberian

Peninsula with the surrender of Granada to King Ferdinand and Queen Isabella. Most people know about the 1492 associated with Columbus and the conquest of the Americas. But few know about this other 1492. For Sephardic Jews, this 1492 is associated with the pain and grief of losing a homeland. That homeland meant so much they continued speaking Spanish, the language of those who expelled them and turned them into wanderers across so many seas. In a way, the Sephardim are similar to many Latinas and Latinos today, who no longer live in their home countries and have become an exiled people who carry their cultural heritage into their new homes and new diasporas.

Researching the history of the Jews in Spain and the expulsion, I found that there was little information about young people and not much at all about girls and young women in that era. I invented the character of Benvenida to imagine what a girl of that time might have thought and felt when banished from her country, a girl who had the tools to articulate her experience, having been taught in secret to read and write by a mother who came from a family of printers.

Skipping from 1492 to 1923, when Reina's story takes place—the section inspired by Abuela's story—might seem strange. Surely I could have created a few more characters between the fifteenth century and the twentieth and twenty-first centuries? I did think of it, but I chose not to. For many people who have a Sephardic heritage, there is this vast gap of time; only a few of us have been able to trace our lineage that far back. But all of us who claim a Sephardic identity have no doubt that our origins are in Spain. Our families spoke Ladino until recently, and many of us carry the names of Spanish towns and cities to this day, like my last name, my father's, Behar, which recalls the Spanish mountain town of Béjar. We also know that much of our history is in our food, a fact confirmed by historians who are finding that Jewish culinary practices from medieval times are preserved in Sephardic kitchens and have become a part of Spanish cuisine.

But where the memory of Sefarad arises in deeply emotional ways for many is in the Sephardic songs, filled with melancholy words and tunes that make you want to cry. Most of these songs are love songs, some dating to medieval times, while others are modern variations. Several songs are alluded to here, but I chose to focus on the song "En la mar hay una torre" (In the sea there is a tower) and have it echo between the sections. This romansa does, indeed, date back to medieval times and contains some of the oldest Ladino we know of. It also has Greek and Roman mythological roots in the figure of the sirens, which some traditions place in the sea near Naples. A song about a maiden in a tower in the middle of the sea might feel like something out of a fairy tale. Yet each of the girls in this book has to negotiate her relationship with the sea and a long heritage of exile, while facing the emotional struggle of growing up and learning who she wants to become.

Sephardic songs reach back into the past in Spain,

and they also draw from influences that have come from dwelling in different lands. Having heard the sad story about my Abuela's oud hanging from a nail in the wall, a story that haunted me for years, I couldn't write this book without incorporating the oud into the story. The oud became an essential part of the Sephardic song tradition because of the intersection of Jewish and Muslim cultures in the Ottoman Empire. I wanted to reflect on the harmony of this musical alliance and how it is fractured by Reina's father, who objects to her friendship with a Muslim boy, Sadik, and sends her away to Cuba. Though this isn't exactly what happened to Abuela, the sorrow of her solitary journey to Cuba with her oud found its way into my imagination.

It occurred to me that we'd see Reina and the next two girls, Alegra and Paloma, all at the same age of twelve, just like Benvenida. Twelve is considered the cusp of adulthood for girls in the Jewish tradition, a year before thirteen, the age for boys. I realized that if these three girls, Reina, Alegra, and Paloma were grandmother, mother, and granddaughter, I'd be able to explore how intergenerational relationships work, what each passes on to the next, what remains of a heritage over the years, and what changes as each of the girls comes of age in a different time and place. While in 1923 Reina is living through the upheaval of Turkey becoming a republic, Alegra in 1961 is in Cuba living through the revolution led by Fidel Castro, and in 2003, Paloma is in Miami coming to terms with all the history that precedes her, both on her father's Afro-Cuban side and on her mother's Sephardic-Cuban side. Paloma's story is meant to break the cycle of departures; her story is about return.

In Spain today, it is possible to travel along the Paths of Sefarad, a network of twenty-two cities that preserve Jewish quarters and different elements of the Sephardic heritage. Thanks to the impressive work of archaeologists and historians, there is increased awareness of the significant traces that remain of the pre-expulsion Jewish presence in the Spanish landscape. That is why I set the ending of this book in the Museo Sefardí of Toledo. This extraordinary museum, housed in a restored fourteenth-century synagogue, has become a mecca for anyone making the pilgrimage to the Sephardic heart of Spain. So it is in the museum that all the stories and all the histories finally converge, from 1492 to the present day of the book. While the museum is real, what happens there is imaginary, so you won't find things like Benvenida's parchment or Sadik's oud if you go, but who knows if one day such a thing might not come true?

I don't know what Abuela would have thought of this book, but I do think she would have liked to be remembered. And she is remembered. She lives on in the cultural heritage she passed on to me in her Spanish that sounded like poetry, her wistful gaze, and the love with which she called me Rutica. Her memory is a blessing, and I am grateful to have shared in these pages the bittersweet beauty of the heritage I inherited from her and my Sephardic family. My hope is that young people of all faiths and backgrounds will gain from this story a new understanding of tolerance and resilience.

Years ago, long after I had no more family left there, I went to Silivri—a city now on the outskirts of Istanbul—and was able to visit the house where Abuela once lived. Rugs hung on the walls; rugs were spread out on the floors. The windows were open, letting in the sea air. I tried to picture her the day she left. I saw her running to the sea. And she didn't look back. She sailed into an unknown world, singing the story that so many years later I heard and wrote down so it would be remembered.

The author's abuela and abuelo, Havana, circa 1928

Sources

Writing a book set in four different locations and in four different time periods led me to read widely about the history of Spain, Turkey, and Cuba, as well as the Cuban exodus to the United States. Below I share some of the sources I drew upon to give historical texture to my novel. In this way, I used my imagination to insert the voices of Benvenida, Reina, Alegra, and Paloma back into history, since the voices of young girls are too often missing in the records of the past. Throughout the book, I refer to all of them as "hijica," the Ladino or Judeo-Spanish word for daughter, as a nod to the unique language that connects them to their Sephardic heritage.

PART ONE

To gain a sense of the lived experience of the expulsion from Spain, I turned to a key source:

The Expulsion 1492 Chronicles: An Anthology of Medieval Chronicles Relating to the Expulsion of the Jews from Spain and Portugal, selected and edited by David Raphael (Carmi House Press, 1992). I also recommend this classic book: *The Jews of Spain: A History of the Sephardic Experience* by Jane S. Gerber (The Free Press, 1992). For a historical novel written for young readers, see Gail Carson Levine's *A Ceiling Made of Eggshells* (HarperCollins, 2020).

The epigraph is drawn from a chronicle written by the priest Andrés Bernáldez, who lived from 1450 to 1513 in the area around Seville. He personally witnessed the exiles making their way to the port at Cádiz. His poignant words can be found, in a slightly different translation, in *The Expulsion 1492 Chronicles*.

The **Edict of Expulsion**, also known as the Alhambra Decree or the Granada Edict, was announced on March 31, 1492. You can find an English translation here: sephardicstudies.org/decree.html.

Rabbi Abraham Senior was born into an important Sephardic family in Segovia in 1412. He became a friend and a close advisor of Queen Isabel, helping to arrange her marriage to King Fernando, who named him the crown rabbi of Castile. Even so, he was unable to convince the king and queen not to order the expulsion of the Jews from Spain. When the time came, he decided to convert instead of leaving the country.

Ten synagogues in Toledo and five Jewish schools. Known as the Sephardic Jerusalem, Toledo was a major center for Jewish life until 1391, a time of pogroms against Jews in Spain. In 1492, by which time many Jews had converted or left, Toledo still had five grand synagogues, two of which remain today, the Sinagoga del Tránsito, now the Sephardic Museum, and Santa María la Blanca, also a museum.

Eggplant. This vegetable became associated with Jewish identity as early as the ninth century when it was introduced to Spain by the

Muslims. There is even a Sephardic "Song of the Eggplants" (Cantiga de las berenjenas).

To learn more:

jewishstudies.washington.edu/converso-cookbook/almodrote-story-behind-recipe

Jews, Food, and Spain: The Oldest Medieval Spanish Cookbook and the Sephardic Culinary Heritage by Hélène Jawhara Piñer (Academic Studies Press, 2022).

Father closes our front door and puts the key inside his robe. I allude here and in part 4 to the Sephardic symbol of the key. As Victor Perera wrote, "When the Jews were expelled from Spain in 1492, many Toledans took with them the keys to their houses. On returning to Toledo centuries later to remove the remains of their ancestors from their old burial plots, the descendants found that their keys still opened the iron-work doors to their former homes." See Perera's book *The Cross and the Pear Tree: A Sephardic Journey* (Knopf, 1995), 38.

Yellow-and-red badges. An edict issued by the pope in 1415 declared that all Jews had to wear badges (described in some sources as yellow with a red center) as a public sign that they had not been baptized into the Catholic faith. This order was generally ignored by kings and Jewish communities alike, but after the Spanish crown issued the Edict of Expulsion in 1492, they began to enforce it as a way to distinguish Jews from those who were not subject to the edict.

¿Por qué no cantas, galana? This was a very old Castilian song that remained popular among Sephardic Jews after the expulsion. The oldest published version dates from the sixteenth century and was republished by the medievalist Diego Catalan (1928–2008) as song 39 in his collection, *El Romancero de la Cuesta del Zarzal*.

Bendigamos al Altisímo. This beloved hymn is sung traditionally as a blessing after meals by Sephardic communities all over the world. It was first mentioned in print in a collection of hymns sung by the Sephardic community in Livorno, Italy, in 1781. I gave myself poetic license and imagined it being sung in 1492 during the expulsion.

Durme, durme. This Sephardic lullaby was recorded in 1943 as sung by Miriam Baruch, a grandmother living in Sophia, Bulgaria, on the eve of the expulsion of the Sephardic community from that city. The recording is archived by the United States Holocaust Memorial Museum here: https://collections.ushmm.org/search/catalog/irn722793.

Show me your face / let me hear your voice / for your voice is sweet / and your face is lovely. This is a biblical verse from Song of Songs 2:14, traditionally sung during the Sephardic synagogue ceremony for welcoming newborn girls into the community.

En la mar hay una torre. According to the composer Martín Kutnowski, this song is "from medieval Spain, originally documented during the first half of the twentieth century by pioneer musicologists Alberto Hemsi and Isaac Levy in locales of the Sephardic Diaspora such as Rhodes, Salonika, Alexandria, and Istanbul" (contrapunctus.com/en_la_mar.htm).

May it be your will, the Almighty, the Great, the Powerful, and the Awesome / That you calm the ocean from its rage and still its waves / That you quickly guide us to our desired destination. These are lines from the "Prayer on Beginning a Sea Voyage," printed in *The Seattle Sephardic Community Daily and Sabbath Siddur*, edited by Isaac Azose (Sephardic Traditions Foundation, 2002), 377.

The Kaddish. This prayer, specifically the form of it known as the Mourner's Kaddish, is recited at Jewish funerals and in every Jewish prayer service. It is a group prayer and by tradition is recited only when at least ten members of the community are present.

Shlomo Ibn Gabirol was a Jewish poet and philosopher from the Caliphate of Córdoba. Also known in Latin translations of his works as Avicebron, he was born in the southern city of Málaga around the year 1021 and died in Valencia some time after 1050. He wrote and published more than one hundred poems in Hebrew and is widely considered the greatest Hebrew poet of the Middle Ages.

PART TWO

Turkish Jews. I learned about the everyday lives of Jews in Turkey through the interviews and oral histories gathered in the Centropa archive (centropa.org/en).

Also recommended: *Sephardi Lives: A Documentary History, 1700–1950*, edited by Julia Phillips Cohen and Sarah Abrevaya Stein (Stanford University Press, 2014).

Tres ermanikas eran. This Sephardic song is derived from the Greek legend of Hero and Leander, in which a father incarcerates his daughter Hero in a tower in the middle of the sea. Her beloved, Leander, swims out to her, guided by the light of the tower, but drowns in the storm-tossed sea. In the Sephardic versions, instead of drowning in the sea, the beloved reaches the tower and is pulled up by Hero's braids. To learn more: Rina Benmayor, "Judeo-Spanish Romansos in Los Angeles," *100 Years of Sephardic Los Angeles*, edited by Sarah Abrevaya Stein and Caroline Luce, UCLA Alan D. Leve Center for Jewish Studies, 2020 (sephardiclosangeles.org/portfolios/judeo-spanish-romansos).

Adio Kerida. A well-known Ladino song of thwarted love, probably composed in the late nineteenth century. Many say it was an adaptation from the last act of Verdi's *La Traviata*.

To learn more: Edwin Seroussi, "Reconstructing Sephardi Music in the 20th Century: Isaac Levy and his '*Chants judeo-espagnols*,'" *The World of Music* 37, no. 1 (1995): 39–58.

PART THREE

Cuban Literacy Campaign. The campaign, led by Fidel Castro, took place over an eighteen-month period, beginning in early 1961, and sought to abolish illiteracy in Cuba. Many young people participated as teachers, including girls from Havana who had never left their families before or visited the countryside.

Catherine Murphy's film offers interviews with female volunteers who participated in the campaign and archival footage from the era (maestrathefilm.org).

Racial tensions during the literacy campaign are mentioned in an oral history found here: *Four Women: Living the Revolution: An Oral History of Contemporary Cuba*, by Oscar Lewis, Ruth M. Lewis, and Susan M. Rigdon (University of Illinois Press, 1977), 66–77.

Fidel Castro's speech: I borrowed from two actual speeches given in 1961. The first paragraph draws on lines from a speech that Castro gave in Havana to party leaders on August 17, 1961. This speech is archived here: lanic.utexas.edu/project/castro/db/1961/19610817.html. The second paragraph comes from a description in *Operation Pedro Pan and the Exodus of Cuba's Children*, by Deborah Shnookal (University of Florida Press, 2020), 70.

Operation Pedro Pan. This program airlifted 14,000 unaccompanied children to the United States in the early 1960s, following the

Cuban revolution. The majority of the children were Catholic, but a few Jewish children were sent out of Cuba as well. One of my cousins was a Pedro Pan child. Among the numerous sources on this topic, I recommend: María de los Angeles Torres, *The Lost Apple: Operation Pedro Pan, Cuban Children in the United States, and the Promise of a Better Future* (Beacon Press, 2003).

PART FOUR

Celia Cruz (1925–2003). Often called the queen of salsa, Celia Cruz became a legendary performer who chose to sing in Spanish as a Cuban exile in the United States. Her legacy is preserved at the Smithsonian Museum (si.edu/spotlight/latin-music-legends-stamps/celia-cruz).

Ladino (Judeo-Spanish): This is a language spoken by Sephardic Jews, comparable to the Yiddish spoken by Ashkenazi Jews. Ladino preserves the Spanish spoken before the departure of the Jews from Spain, with the addition of many words from other languages acquired in the Diaspora. It's written traditionally in the letters of the Hebrew alphabet and in modern times in the Roman alphabet. To mark its difference, the spelling is different in Ladino than in Spanish. For example, instead of the qu used in Spanish, Ladino uses the letter *k*—so *querida* becomes *kerida*. Scholars as well as singers from around the world, including Rachel Bortnick, Rina Benmayor, Devin Naar, Bryan Kirschen, Karen Sarhon, Susana Behar, Liliana Benveniste, and Sarah Aroeste, are working to maintain and revitalize Ladino.

To learn more:

sephardicstudies.org/komunita.html

ladinolinguist.com

jewishstudies.washington.edu/sephardic-studies

esefarad.com

Federico García Lorca (1898–1936) was one of the greatest poets and playwrights of his generation. His 1935 poem "Llanto por Ignacio Sánchez Mejías," sometimes translated as "Lament for the Death of a Bullfighter," is considered one of the best elegies in the Spanish language. Lorca was murdered in August 1936, at the outset of the Spanish Civil War. His killers are thought to have been supporters of the right-wing coup leaders who began the war, though his death was never properly investigated. A statue in honor of Lorca, depicting the poet holding a songbird (either a lark or a nightingale) between his hands, was installed in the Plaza de Santa Ana in the center of Madrid in the 1990s.

The Museo Sefardí (The Sephardic Museum) of Toledo was built by the Spanish government in the 1960s as an annex to the fourteenth-century Synagogue of El Tránsito, in the heart of the ancient Jewish quarter of Toledo. It opened in 1971 and has continued to collect more artifacts of the Jewish presence in Spain ever since (though the poem on parchment that figures in this story is entirely fictional!). The marble basin mentioned in the text was found in the city of Tarragona and dates to the fifth century. It is inscribed with the words *Peace upon Israel and upon all of us and our children* in Hebrew, as well as the word *peace* in Latin and Greek. You can see an image of it on the Museo Sefardí web site: culturaydeporte.gob.es/msefardi/colecciones/piezas-destacadas/pileta.html.

Acknowledgments

I am immensely grateful to Nancy Paulsen for believing in this book and believing I could write it. Nancy traveled with me every step of the way on the imaginative journey from Spain to Turkey to Cuba to Miami and back to Spain. She is a profound reader and editor, and the best doula of stories struggling to be born. I feel truly blessed to have worked with her again. I can't thank you enough, Nancy. I owe you lots of Toledo marzipan and so much more!

My agent, Alyssa Eisner Henkin, stood by me, offering unwavering encouragement, patience, and loving support as this book took form, as she has done since I began writing creative works for young readers. From that first reply to my query nine years ago to this day, I feel incredibly lucky that our paths converged. Thank you, Alyssa. I truly appreciate all you've done to help my books find a home in the world.

I want to thank all the writer friends who took time from their busy lives to read early drafts of this book. To Marjorie Agosin, for urging me to write poetically. To Lucía Suárez, for pointing out the strengths to build upon. To Reyna Grande, for a deep critical reading that led me to make essential revisions. To Sandra Cisneros, for brainstorming titles with me and gracing me with kind words as I finished this book. To Rosa Lowinger, for essential moral support. To Ana Menendez, for sharing her Miami stories with me. To Richard Blanco, for always reminding me of how poetry lives in us.

I was fortunate to be able to turn to several experts in Sephardic studies for advice about how to represent the songs, the culture, and the history of Sephardic people. Early on, a conversation with Jane Gerber lit a spark that allowed me to begin this book. Teo Ruiz shared his vast knowledge of medieval Spain that helped me create a more accurate picture of the 1492 expulsion. Dalia Kandiyoti gave me suggestions that helped me envision the Turkish setting more clearly. Rina Benmayor offered me wisdom about the Sephardim and their journeys. A correspondence with Judith Cohen gave me insights into the complex history of the Sephardic song repertoire. And to Hannah Pressman, I want to give an especially big thank-you for reading an early and a later draft of this book and offering me generous comments on the whole story as well as a rich mythological and historical understanding of the song about the girl in the tower.

By the summer of 2022, I had a complete draft of the book, but I felt a need to return to Toledo and see it and experience it again. I was so glad to be able to make this journey with my husband, David, and two fellow Cuban friends, Jesús Jambrina and Alfredo Alonso Estenoz, and together explore the Sephardic traces still so alive in that Spanish city. We ate eggplants that tasted heavenly there. It was magical to set foot in the Museo Sefardí yet again, and this time to be received by its director, Carmen Álvarez Nogales, who offered us a warm welcome. And I was glad for the gracious company of Marifé Andrés Andrés, who gave me a great Jewish archaeological tour of Toledo in 2019 that inspired me to set the story there.

The passion that many Spaniards now feel for the Jewish past of Spain seems amazing to me, and even more so their desire to enact Jewish traditions today. I have witnessed this fascinating turn toward everyday reparative acts among the members of Zamora Sefardí, an organization promoting Sephardic scholarship founded by Jesús and Alfredo. Though not Jewish, many feel it their responsibility to celebrate Shabbat and Jewish holidays, and they search for traces of the Jewish past with a great sense of commitment. In turn, the impressive work carried out by the Centro Sefarad-Israel in Madrid, under the leadership of Esther Bendahan Cohen, has shone a light on the many literary and cultural possibilities for both preserving and enlivening the Sephardic presence in Spain.

Having been a traveler to Spain now for nearly half a century, and having spent many years of my youth living there in a small village, it has been nothing short of miraculous to experience the way the Paths of Sefarad have become such a vibrant and visible part of the landscape and the culture. I remember when I first went to the town of Béjar in the mountains near Salamanca as a young woman, wondering if there was any connection to our family name, Behar. But there was no one to ask, no one to speak to about the memory of the Jewish presence. And now there is a Jewish museum in Béjar. I had the good fortune in the summer of 2022 to visit it again and want to thank Carmen Rubio for her enthusiastic work as director of the Museo Judío de Béjar. I was honored to find a VHS copy of my documentary, *Adio Kerida/Goodbye Dear Love*, kept in a glass exhibition case like an heirloom.

I want to thank John Parra for his beautiful cover artwork. The image beautifully conveys the search for new beginnings of Benvenida, Reina, Alegra, and Paloma.

I am grateful to Brian Luster, Cindy Howle, Ariela Rudy Zaltzman, and Kathleen Keating for doing a terrific job on the copyediting. Also thanks to Sara LaFleur for assisting with the editing from start to finish, and making sure all went well with the bookmaking process. Thanks to Marikka Tamura and Kristin Boyle for the lovely work on the design of the book. It's a pleasure to work with so many of the extraordinary teams at Penguin Random House, and I'd especially like to thank everyone in the educational and marketing departments.

A warm thank-you to all the teachers, librarians, booksellers, and readers who have connected with my stories and given me the confidence to keep writing.

I wrote this book in memory of my paternal grandmother, Rebeca, to honor her story, and to honor the Sephardic heritage that she and my grandfather, Isaac, passed on to my father and our family. I am grateful to them for sharing a minority identity that might easily have disappeared if not for their everyday commitment to preserving the language of Ladino, and Sephardic food traditions, proverbs, and folklore.

Gracias to Papi, who adores Sephardic songs, and gracias to Mami, who learned to cook so deliciously in the Sephardic style to please Papi. Their love for the Sephardic legacy has been an inspiration. And gracias to Tía Fanny, who has shared many intriguing family stories and offers me borekas and bulemas when I visit her in Miami.

I thank David, my husband and friend, for everything he does to make it possible for me to live and write and stay healthy and sane. Much of this book was written during the scariest moments of the pandemic years, and we got through that time together with a renewed sense of purpose and love of life. David read several drafts of this book and helped with fact-checking, locating sources, and figuring out things like a possible route on foot from Toledo to Valencia in 1492. I am glad he was with me for the imagined and the real journeys to Spain, which in the end came together in unexpected ways in this book.

I thank Gabriel, my son, as always, for all the joys and blessings he has given me, among them taking an interest in his Sephardic heritage. I thank Sasha, my daughter-in-law, for her kindness, generosity, and openness of spirit. And I am also so grateful to Gabriel and Sasha for bringing two delightful granddaughters into the world. I look forward to the day when Mila and Colette will read this book and ask about their ancestors.

Ruth Behar
Ann Arbor, March 2023